בה

Saba UNDER *the* HYENA'S FOOT

GIRLS *of* MANY LANDS

England ⇻ 1592
Isabel: Taking Wing by Annie Dalton

France ⇻ 1711
Cécile: Gates of Gold by Mary Casanova

Turkey ⇻ 1720
Leyla: The Black Tulip by Alev Lytle Croutier

Ethiopia ⇻ 1846
Saba: Under the Hyena's Foot by Jane Kurtz

China ⇻ 1857
Spring Pearl: The Last Flower by Laurence Yep

Yup'ik Alaska ⇻ 1890
Minuk: Ashes in the Pathway by Kirkpatrick Hill

Ireland ⇻ 1937
Kathleen: The Celtic Knot by Siobhán Parkinson

India ⇻ 1939
Neela: Victory Song by Chitra Banerjee Divakaruni

Saba UNDER *the* HYENA'S FOOT

by Jane Kurtz

Published by Pleasant Company Publications
Copyright © 2003 by Pleasant Company

Visit our Web site at **americangirl.com**

Printed in China.
03 04 05 06 07 08 09 C&C 10 9 8 7 6 5 4 3 2 1

Girls of Many Lands™, Saba™, and American Girl®
are trademarks of Pleasant Company.

PERMISSIONS & PICTURE CREDITS

The following individuals and organizations have generously given permission to reprint illustrations contained in "Then and Now": pp. 197—© Carol Beckwith-Angela Fisher/Robert Estall Agency UK (Gondar, Ethiopia); pp. 198–199—© Roger Wood/CORBIS (house); © Victor Englebert (girl with water jug); Mary Evans Picture Library (Gondar palaces); pp. 200–201—The British Museum, Dept. of Ethnography (1993.AF16.1a) (kemis); Oleg Svyatoslavsky/Life File (women in shammas); © Werner Forman/CORBIS (necklace); © Jon Hicks/CORBIS (angels); pp. 202–203—*Solomon and the Queen of Sheba* (detail) by James Tissot, Jewish Museum, New York City / © SuperStock; © Caroline Penn/Panos Pictures (health education class); © Victor Englebert (Amhara girls).

Illustration by Jean-Paul Tibbles
Title Calligraphy by Linda P. Hancock

Library of Congress Cataloging-in-Publication Data
Kurtz, Jane.
Saba : under the hyena's foot / by Jane Kurtz ;
illustration by Jean-Paul Tibbles.
p. cm. — (Girls of many lands)
"American Girl."
Summary: After being kidnapped and brought to the emperor's palace in Gondar, Ethiopia, twelve-year-old Saba discovers that she and her brother are part of the emperor's desperate attempt to consolidate political power in 1846.
ISBN 1-58485-747-1 (pbk.) — 1-58485-829-X (hc)
1. Ethiopia—History—19th century—Juvenile fiction.
[1. Ethiopia—History—19th century—Fiction.
2. Kings, queens, rulers, etc.—Fiction. 3. Kidnapping—Fiction.
4. Brothers and sisters—Fiction.]
I. Tibbles, Jean-Paul, ill. II. Title. III. Series.
PZ7.K9626 Sab 2003 [Fic]—dc21 2002155613

For Yohannes, *whose determination and vision make dreams spring out of ashes*

Acknowledgments:
I'm deeply grateful to Dr. Richard Pankhurst, not only for reading this manuscript but also for writing so many books full of details about Ethiopian history. I'm also thankful for all the Ethiopian chroniclers and European visitors who took time to record what they saw and experienced in Ethiopia. The Straw Umbrella *by Dana Faralla gave me several great ideas. Yohannes Gebregeorgis and Hanna Taffessa helped me with some obscure bits of cultural research. And what would I do without my mom, lifelong avid reader and collector of books about Ethiopia? I used her copy of* King of Kings: Tewodros of Ethiopia *by Sven Rubenson as my definitive source about some confusing relationships and dates.*

Contents

Saba's Family Tree

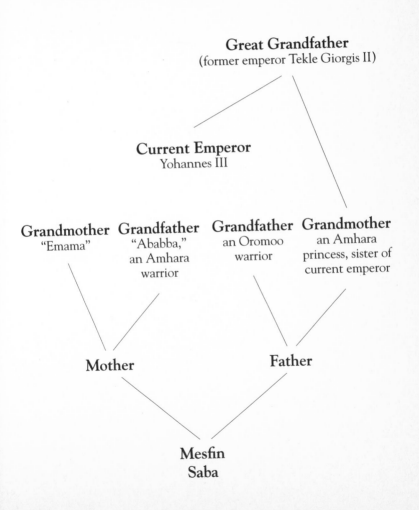

Great Grandfather
(former emperor Tekle Giorgis II)

Current Emperor
Yohannes III

Grandmother
"Emama"

Grandfather
"Ababba,"
an Amhara
warrior

Grandfather
an Oromoo
warrior

Grandmother
an Amhara
princess, sister of
current emperor

Mother

Father

**Mesfin
Saba**

1 *Fear and Disaster*

I stopped, rocking slightly on my bare feet in the cold mud at the edge of the stream. My heart was flapping as wildly as a piece of cloth caught in the wind. The strange little song came again from the forest. A *zar*. It must be a zar because how could anything except a spirit sing with such haunting, honeyed sweetness?

I tried to peer into the trees that grew close together, shoulder to shoulder, an army of trees that I thought someday might tear up their own roots and march off to serve one of the faraway emperors. Mist from the day's rain was draped over the branches.

Something heavy crashed in the woods for a moment and was still. I felt the skin on the back of my neck quiver. A leopard? Or maybe something even

worse. Water and forest were two of the places where
Saytan lived, evil and black as deep darkness, with
eyes of fire and horns poking up behind his ears.
Emama, my grandmother, said so. Emama knew
all there was to know about such things.

"*Ayezosh*," I whispered to myself. *Have courage.*
I picked up a stone that curved into the palm of my
hand. It wasn't much of a weapon, but I knew I could
throw it with all my strength. I moved down the slope.
My feet slipped on the wet clay. I caught myself and
crouched by the stream.

Balancing our huge pot against some roots that
jutted out from the bank, I used a gourd to scoop and
scoop the cold water into the pot. My older brother,
Mesfin, often said, "A coward sweats even in water,"
but I could feel no sweat on my toes—even though
I knew I was a coward.

When the water reached the top of the narrow neck
of the pot, I reluctantly dropped the rock, watching it
splash into the stream. I straightened against the
smooth, curved clay of the pot and hoisted it with
both hands carefully onto my back. A leather strap

wound through both handles. I slipped the strap over my head and shrugged my shoulders until I felt the leather tight against my chest.

Then I climbed the bank on unsteady feet. Took two steps. A breeze whirled, lifting my ragged skirt to flutter around my ankles. The breeze brought a smell of something strange—something mysterious and pungent. I began to walk quickly away from the stream. *Don't look*, I told myself, but I couldn't help a frightened peek over my shoulder.

That's when my foot caught on a root.

"Blessed Mariam help me!" I cried out, but the holy mother didn't reach down with any miracle. The heavy pot pushed me forward, and I fell to my hands and knees on the wet ground. Frantically, I groped behind me with one hand, trying to hold the pot in place, but I could feel it sliding as water splashed out and over me. No! It thudded heavily to the ground with a cracking sound that made me wince. Emama said, "One rock is useless to keep a hundred baboons from the corn, but it can shatter a hundred pots."

I didn't have a hundred pots. Emama, Mesfin, and

I had only this one, and a rock had definitely shattered it, leaving me kneeling in a puddle of water.

Something splashed softly in the stream behind me, and I didn't wait to see whether it was just a frog or something worse. I slid the leather strap over my head, scrambled to my feet—not bothering to pick up the pieces of shiny black clay—and ran toward the house as fast as though Saytan himself were trying to pinch my heels.

The path twisted three times, shook itself free of trees, and there! Just ahead was the fence that Ababba, my grandfather, had made from dry thorn branches. Beyond that, at the top of a small rise, was our house. I slowed a little, panting, and glanced around. The ground where we grew our food was still mostly red mud. Soon it would be time for Mesfin to plow the earth again and drop barley and chickpea seeds into the ground.

I stopped and listened. Nothing seemed to be following. I sniffed carefully, but this time I smelled nothing strange.

From somewhere in the forest, a hyena's whoop

drifted through the late afternoon air. That was odd. Hyenas rarely came out before dark. I ran the rest of the way to the house, stooped through the low doorway, and stumbled forward, kneeling to throw my arms around Emama's knees.

"What is it, Saba, my child?" Emama's voice was silky and old, full of the strength of many years. She had borne much sorrow. Her daughter—my mother—was dead. Her daughter's husband—my father—was dead. And now, Ababba had also died. She and Ababba had made homes for us in three different places, each one far from any village, "so that no one can find us to hurt us" was all she would ever say. Sometimes she added, "If anything dangerous does come our way, don't forget that your grandfather was a great warrior in his time. He will protect us."

So, without Ababba, were we as helpless as featherless baby birds? I shivered.

"What has brought fear to your stomach? Tell me." Emama put her spinning down. Her voice was calm, but I was almost sure I could hear anxiety rippling beneath the calmness.

I told the story, trying to make my voice copy the strange notes I had heard in the forest. "Do you think it was a zar?"

"Possibly it was just a bird," Emama said cautiously. "Or perhaps a zar in the shape of a bird." Then she went on with her usual warnings. I must never go into the thickest part of the forest because Saytan liked to lurk there, as well as in deep water, caves, and dirty places. If Mesfin or I ever saw any stranger approach, we must hide, in case it was a barbarian or even a *buda*, a person who had the power to drink our blood through the magic of the evil eye. We mustn't eat outside because loose zar spirits could fly into our bodies, bringing sickness or seizures. "Whatever you heard in the forest," Emama finished, "I will need to go to the market tomorrow to replace the pot. I will also see if I can find an amulet to protect you from any zar."

"May Mesfin and I go with you, to help you?" I scooped Emama's hand between both of mine and kissed it.

"No," she said, just as I was afraid she would.

"I think it better to have you and Mesfin stay here, inside the house. With your grandfather gone, we must be careful. After all, who now will protect us?"

"I will." The sudden voice made me gasp. I had to stop myself from burying my head in Emama's skirts, as I used to when I was a child.

Before I could do anything so foolish, I realized it was just Mesfin, who had come into the house on silent feet. "I will fight any strangers that come," he said in his voice that was still a boy's voice even though he was now almost as tall as Ababba had been. He was older than I was, but not by much.

He made a fierce face at Emama. "You and Saba can hide in the bushes while I chase all of them away." His bare feet thudded on the hard mud floor as he leaped forward and backward, slashing a stick as if it were a sword and making fierce grunts.

Emama clicked her tongue. "Such foolish talk. No, you will stay inside tomorrow, my little spiders. You have no understanding of how strange and fearsome this world can be."

Mesfin stopped his leaping about, but he did not put

the stick down.

Emama got carefully to her feet. "Blow on the fire," she told me. "I myself will look around outside to see if any odd sound seizes my ears. If I hear nothing, I will prepare our supper." She bent over and disappeared awkwardly through the low doorway. Since Ababba's death, she had begun to walk more slowly and with a stoop to her shoulders.

"She must let us go with her to the market," I told Mesfin. I could hear my voice tremble as I forced out the next words. "What if she doesn't come back?"

"Spiders," Mesfin muttered. In a perfect imitation of Emama's voice, he added the saying she was so fond of: "When spiders unite, they can tie up a lion."

I crouched by the fire, poking at the coals to see which ones had alive red eyes under their gray coverings. "This spider," I said, "is never going to even *see* a lion and certainly will never help to tie one up." I leaned over and blew on the coals. Fire glowed to life.

Maybe Emama could dig a clay pit near the stream and we could make a new pot by ourselves. No, that was foolish thinking. The only people who could make pots were budas, who knew how to put an evil eye on people. Emama was certainly no buda.

"She should be back by now," Mesfin said impatiently. "I'm going after her. If something dangerous is out there, she will need me by her side."

I glanced fearfully toward the door. Was there still light outside? When sunset galloped across the sky, it pulled the plow of darkness right behind it.

Suddenly, Emama filled the doorway, and relief fluttered in me. Without a word, Emama walked over, crouched by the fire, and moved the gourd filled with *injera* batter closer to the fire. She put the griddle on the stones so that it perched over the fire like a huge circle, as round and flat as the world. Emama rubbed the griddle with a cloth dipped in oil. Then she poured the batter.

I hurried to help. She must not have seen anything terrible because she had come back to make our food. As I watched, the injera grew eyes—hundreds of little eyes staring up at me. I put the clay top over the griddle, then removed it. Emama loosened the big injera pancake with hands so leathery that they didn't seem to feel the heat. We might not have meat for our *wat*, but the injera would be fresh and delicious.

She laid the injera carefully on the basket. Emama and Ababba used to eat first, with Mesfin and me eating after. Now, with Ababba gone, we all ate together. Emama was food and warmth and comfort. I wanted to be near her always.

"Don't go," I whispered, so softly I was almost sure she could not hear me. "Or if you do go, take us with you."

2 A Fierce Longing

The house grew cold as we ate, and I heard the wind drumming with its fingers against our grass roof. Emama, Mesfin, and I all pulled our *shammas* tightly around our shoulders.

Luckily, the month of *Maskaram* was almost upon us, when the big rains would lift their wet, heavy hands from around the earth's neck. Streams and rivers would shrink back to their normal size. Fields would wiggle to life again. Evenings would shed some of their chill.

Since the beginning of the rainy season, Mesfin and I had gone about our work huddled under capes we had woven from reeds. Almost every day, Emama told me, "Saba, you look like a turtle, carrying your house around with you wherever you go." We coughed and shivered as we pushed our way through rain and wet, cold mud. But soon the dark clouds would come no more. The *kosso* trees would sprout red flames. In the fields, *maskal* flowers would make a thick yellow cloak for my bare feet to walk on. Sunshine, as bright and lovely as a hundred lemons, would fill up the sky.

Questions swirled inside of me as I tore off a piece of injera and scooped up a bite of the spicy lentil wat Emama had prepared. Why didn't she want to take us with her to the market? What did she fear? My stomach was almost full of lentils and cabbage and an unfamiliar feeling—a fierce longing to go with Emama. *Just to help her,* I told myself. But deep down I knew I also wanted to see the market for myself.

Twice, long ago, I had been a traveler. The first time, when I was little more than an infant, we had left the land the emperor had given Ababba and moved to the land of Ababba's fathers. The second time, we moved to this place on the edge of the wild forest. Here, Ababba had to build a house. I watched him cut down a tree for the center pole and smaller trees to put in a circle around it. After he had dug a pit of clay, I helped stomp the clay to softness and then mixed straw into it. Then we all scooped up handfuls of clay and used it to build the walls.

Emama and Ababba had never spoken of why we had moved and why we lived so far from other people. Often those questions buzzed inside of me. But I would never upset my grandparents by asking. "Who taught you to be rude?" Ababba would have said. "It is not a child's place to question elders."

We had almost everything we needed here. Seeds that we pressed for the oil we used in cooking. A cow that gave us milk to make into butter. An ox to pull the plow. Red peppers to spice our food. Gourds and baskets for scooping and storing. The few other things we needed, such as an iron plow blade or a pot—both of which were made by budas—Ababba had fetched from some market or other when he rode out on his mule for his yearly travels.

So what was this restless stirring inside of me? Perhaps it had to do with what Mesfin had said yesterday. I swallowed embarrassment as I remembered his words. "Why are you teaching her to make flour?" he had asked Emama as I knelt beside her in the house, pushing the grinding stone against the large, smooth rock. "Is it because soon she will have a husband to feed with the strength of her arms?"

My mouth opened, but my throat found no words. Fortunately, Emama spoke quickly. "Stop that talk. She's very small, yet."

"But . . ."

"No more." Her tone was sharp. "It will take all three of us to grow enough food to help us survive the next dry season."

Full of relief, I had picked up a little coarse flour and rubbed it between my fingers. "I'm not ever leaving here," I had said. "This is my home." The little I knew about other places came from Ababba's stories and the paintings in the goatskin book that Emama showed us on feast days. I also had a few memories from our travels—a far-off glimpse of great water that Ababba called Lake Dembya, a village market where I once held amber beads like pools of melted butter in my hand and played with another little girl. Couldn't even someone who loved her home want to see the glories of the world just for one day?

Every time Ababba went away and came home, he told stories of the many different markets he had visited. The salt market in Mekelle, where salt dust dried his lips and turned the skin on his arms to white. Magnificent Gondar, where he traded for foreign red cloth that a weaver unraveled and used to make a red border for a feast-day shamma. A place near Lake Dembya, where Ababba found cotton and lemons to bring home to us.

I had always liked to say the names of these faraway places. Now, as I stared at the dying embers of the fire, I admitted to myself that I wanted to see just one market again.

"I will need to set out early in the morning," Emama said. "The two of you must stay inside all day. Do not leave this house until you hear me coming back."

Mesfin made a low, disgusted sound, and Emama turned to scold him.

I looked anxiously from one to the other, so unsettled by my brother's behavior that I blurted out the words that flew into my mouth. "Perhaps you want to keep all the marvels for yourself."

"Don't be disrespectful." Emama's face was full of thunder. "Anyone would think your mother forgot to give you butter and honey when you were born to make your voice soft and sweet. Don't forget. It is better to have a foot that slips than a tongue that slips."

I looked down at the floor. "I'm sorry." But Emama's words made me ache to be even more disrespectful and let more questions come pouring out. Did my mother truly give me butter and honey when I was born? Or was death already bragging in her ear even as she held me for the first time?

"Yes," Emama grumbled on. "You may well be sorry. I go to buy a pot, not amber beads to hang around my neck."

For a moment, it was as if I were holding the yellow-gold glossy beads in my hand again. Amber could also be red. "That color," Ababba had told me, pointing with his chin to a deep red sun that was about to kiss the world good-bye and go into its dark shell for the night. "Someday," he added, "I will find just the right amber beads to bring home for you."

As I lifted my last bite of wat and injera to my

mouth, I sneaked a quick look. Was Emama still
angry? Or upset? I couldn't tell. Her wrinkled face
didn't give any of her thoughts away. She kept her
counsel to herself.

Without warning, Emama reached out and pulled
me closer to her. After a moment, I felt her fingers in
my hair. I closed my eyes. She hummed softly, almost
under her breath, as she began to pull and tug at my
hair, undoing and redoing the tiny braids. At first, I
squirmed, pulling my head to this side or that, trying
to escape those little stabs of pain on my scalp. I patted
Emama's knee. "Perhaps you are going to the village
Ababba told us about," I said carefully. "The one with
the big tree in the middle."

Emama gave my hair a sharp tug. "There are many
trees in this world."

"But this tree had butter rubbed into its trunk,"
I said. "Because of the sacred snake that lived in the
tree. Ababba said sometimes an elder kills a goat or
sheep and leaves it there for the snake to eat." What
I did not say was that I wanted to stand before this tree
and ask for protection for Emama, Mesfin, and me

now that Ababba was gone. I wanted it even more than I wanted to hold amber beads in my hand again.

"A snake." Emama sniffed, and I knew she was not pleased. "What are you? A hippopotamus-eater to believe such tales?" Her words made me cringe. Had I said something so terrible that my own grandmother compared me to people who ate the unclean meat of a hippopotamus? Stubbornly, I still wondered if a sacred snake *did* have power against all the terrible things of the real world and maybe even the spirit world.

"Are you forgetting your *Amhara* blood?" Emama asked sharply. "And your name?" Then her voice softened. "Long, long ago," she began, "the Amhara people worshiped many things—trees, snakes, the sun. But no more. Have I told you this story?"

"Yes, Emama," I whispered.

"One snake became so powerful," Emama went on, "that the people had to feed it each day—ten cows and ten bulls, a thousand goats, a hundred sheep, and ten thousand of ten thousand of birds."

As Emama spoke, her fingers gradually became more gentle, and I relaxed. I knew this story well—in fact,

Emama and Ababba both had their own versions they
liked to tell. I liked Emama's way, where the snake
had eyes of fiery flame and black eyebrows and a horn.
Emama made me see the woman, Makeda, who had
astonishing courage. She walked right up to the snake,
looked him over, and then cut off his head. Ababba
said it was Makeda's father who cut off the head, but
Emama thought differently.

I sighed. Even in the story that the Amharas told
of their own ancient beginnings, snakes were powerful.
Were they the most powerful things in the world?
No, Makeda was more powerful than the snake—and,
as it turned out, even she was not the most powerful
thing in all the earth, or the water, fire, and air beneath
it. Emama was now telling this part.

After the Ethiopian people made Makeda queen—
Queen of Saba—she heard about someone who had
great wisdom, even more wisdom than she had. So she
took seven hundred ninety camels and many mules
and donkeys and went on a long journey in the
burning heat of the sun until she found King Solomon
of Israel. While they walked and talked in the king's

palace, she saw that the light of the king's heart was like a lamp in the darkness. On her way home, with Solomon's son growing inside of her, she declared that her people—our people, the Amhara—would not worship snakes or the sun anymore but only the one true God. All the Ethiopian emperors were descended from her.

"And you carry the name of Saba, that great queen." Emama finished the story and my hair at the same time. She cupped my face in her strong hands and turned my head this way and that with a look of satisfaction. "Your head is now beautiful, praise be to God."

Mesfin laughed. "It looks like a field just plowed." I laughed with him, but under my laughter I could again feel prickles of fear. I thought of Ababba harnessing the ox and walking slowly behind, while the plow made the red earth curl. Could Mesfin do it all by himself now? Without my brother's help, would I alone be able to throw enough stones to keep the monkeys, birds, and baboons out of the fields once the crops came up?

Emama stood up and hung our baskets and gourds
on the cow horns Ababba had fixed into the mud walls
of the house. Mesfin and I stepped outside, where the
moon was rising to give us a little light, and guided the
animals through a special door in the back of our small
house. Four chickens. Two goats. The cow. The ox that
would pull the plow. Ababba's mule used to come in
here, too, but he had died two months before his
master did.

When the animals were tethered in their usual
places, I moved over to the corner of the floor where
I always slept and curled up in my *gahbi*. Emama
settled on a bench of mud that jutted out from the
wall and that was covered with animal hides and
straw to make a little softness for her old bones.

As I listened to the chickens rustling on their
perches, I thought again about the strange crawling
in my stomach when Emama had said "your mother."
I wished I could whisper now to Mesfin, the way we
had talked sometimes when we sat for hours on the
platform in the field, throwing stones at monkeys and
birds. I wanted to ask him again if he had any memory

of our parents' faces. But no. I shut my eyes, feeling mournful and alone. He had told me many times that the only thing he remembered was a babble of many voices and a fearful wailing.

Most of the time, we spoke to our grandparents and thought of them as if they were our parents. Had we not been with them since we were little children? But now Emama's words had set off such a longing in me. When Emama comes back from the market, I must find a way to coax her to tell me about my mother and father. As I tried to settle on the hard mud floor, the longing bubbled in me like a river. I had to know more.

3 Fire in the Night

I felt as if I had been asleep for only a few minutes
when the squawking of the chickens startled me
awake. In the darkness, I heard scrambling sounds.
I sat up, clutching my gahbi so tightly that I could
almost feel my own fingernails through the thick cloth.
"Emama!" It was Mesfin's voice coming from outside.
"Come quickly."

For a moment, I stuck my head under the gahbi and
curled up as small as a spider on the wall, one of the
ones that sat so still, hoping to escape the searching
lizard's tongue. Maybe this voice was only a dream.

"Saba!" My emama's call was loud and commanding.

Ayezosh, I told myself. The lizard usually got the
spiders whether they sat still or whether they ran. I
shook off the gahbi, scurried to the door, and stuck

my head out. In the thorn fence, I saw the flickering orange of small flames.

"We could run that way." Mesfin pointed with his chin. "Toward the stream."

"No." Emama's voice was firm. "Saba, bring me some coals from the fire. Here. Take these."

Even in my hurry, I remembered to reach out both hands in the polite way. I took the broad leaf and twig that Emama was holding out, pulled my head inside, took a step backward, tripped over a chicken, and fell. I could hear the restless stamping of feet, the flapping of wings, and the mutterings of animal voices. I could even smell their fear.

Not bothering to stand up again, I crawled toward the place where the fire lived. When my fingers touched one of the warm stones Emama used for balancing the griddle, I blew urgently until a coal glowed orange in the darkness.

I used the twig to push the coal onto the leaf and then rushed back outside.

"Over here." Emama looked like some spirit creature, her face half-lit with moonlight, half-dark with shadow. She hastily piled little pieces of straw onto the coal. *What?* We already had too much fire.

Mesfin loomed out of the darkness and grabbed my hand. "You can help me."

We hurried off. "But what is Emama doing?" I was trotting to keep up with him, hoping I wouldn't smash my foot on a rock.

"If necessary, she will make a second fire to run toward the first fire and bite it. But she will do that only if she must, to save the house and the animals." He paused for a moment to strip a branch from a tree in one swift motion. "If God is willing, you and I can keep the fire from getting near."

"How?" We were now close enough that I could hear the crackling laughter of the fire where it danced in the dry thorns. Closer. Closer. Now I felt its heat on my face.

Mesfin lifted the branch and began to beat the sparks that flew from the fire. More boldly, he slapped at the edges where the fire flickered toward us. "Pull off a branch," he told me, his voice coming out in gasps.

I lunged at the nearest tree and yanked off a green

branch, forcing myself not to shrink away when the rough bark tore my hands. Then, giving a huge cry, I began to beat the fire. I imagined I was Makeda and this was the terrible snake. One of us had to die. "Not me," I panted, hitting the fire over and over. "Not me."

I hardly knew what I was doing until I felt Mesfin's hand on my shoulder and heard his voice. "I think we have conquered this fire." He prodded a charred piece of the fence with his branch but no flame leaped out at him. "You see." His voice was full of pride and maybe just a little anger. "Emama thinks we are children, but we were strong enough to beat back the fire. Now she knows that we can take care of ourselves and need not stay huddled in our house. I think she will let us go to the market."

4 Call of the Honey Bird

But Mesfin was wrong. When I woke, coughing, I saw that Emama was prodding the embers, coaxing them into flame with her breath. "Praise to God who brought you safely through this night," she said when I sat up. "In this gourd is a little roasted grain that you may eat this day. Now fetch your ababba's walking stick for me."

The smell of smoke was thicker than usual, filling up my head. I looked at my poor, stinging hands. Why were these terrible things suddenly coming upon us? First the pot and now a fire. Had some buda stumbled onto our isolated home, just as Emama had always warned us? A buda could make bad things happen just by thinking about them.

"Hurry," she said. I rushed to do what she told me.

She stood up, clutching her hip, clicking her tongue, and muttering. "I wonder what might cause a fire," she finally said aloud, perhaps to Mesfin or perhaps to herself.

"There was no lightning," Mesfin said.

"No lightning." Emama studied the underside of the grass roof. "I could take you with me where you would be under my watchful eye."

My stomach sang yes. *Yes*.

"No," she decided. "If some buda is about, you will be safer here in the house. Do not take the animals to graze today," she told Mesfin. "Tie them up just outside, here. Do not leave this house."

We watched as she took a salt bar that was wrapped in a piece of cloth and hidden in a basket in the corner. She would use the salt to pay for the pot and anything else we needed. Emama was now mother *and* father to us, and I wondered what we could do to get more salt to buy the things we needed.

When she looked over at me, she must have seen the worry in my eyes, because she said, "Ayezosh. After the salt is gone, I know how to make other things to trade at the market. I will fix kosso flowers in a way that will cure the worms that rich people get from the delicious raw meat they eat. I can make a medicine for coughing, too, out of honey and certain pressed seeds."

We said good-bye in the traditional way of greeting and parting, lips to cheeks, over and over. I wanted to cling to her, but I knew I must not. "Ayezosh," she said again. "Grind a little grain the way I showed you. Play the *gebeta* game with Mesfin."

To Mesfin, she said, "You know the saying—smoke and a boy both disappear and no one knows how they do it. You must make a lie of this saying. Do not leave your sister alone."

Then she was gone.

I helped Mesfin take the animals outside, chasing a stubborn chicken that squawked and fluttered around the room. After we had gathered grass for the animals to eat, we went back inside, as Emama had said we must. I put a handful of grain in the middle of the large stone and picked up the second stone. My hands were sore, but I kept pushing. When the grain turned to flour, it fell into a basin at the foot of the large stone.

I looked over at Emama's spindle. Before I was big enough to fetch water from the stream, I used to clean seeds from the cotton she spun into thread. When I was a little older, I learned how to spin. For a long time, though, I had been so busy helping pull weeds or throw stones or carry water that I didn't have time for such things. Emama did the spinning by herself, taking three or four months to fill enough spindles with thread for a shamma. Then Ababba would take the thread to the weavers. The weavers, he said, sat at wooden looms, sometimes with holes dug for their feet, and it appeared to him somewhat magical the way they could take thread and turn it into cloth.

I flipped the edge of my shamma where it had fallen off my shoulder. It had only a thin border. Ababba said that the shammas of the rich people had thick, fancy borders created out of silks from India and Syria— countries far, far away. The weavers unraveled the foreign threads to create their own patterns of blue and yellow and red. "Someday," he would say, "I will bring a soft, beautiful shamma for you, to take the place of this rough one." Now that day would never come.

I was considering whether I should do some spinning when Mesfin said casually, "Yesterday, when I was out with the goats, I heard the cry of a honey bird."

His voice did not fool me. I studied him carefully to see what he was trying to say. This small brown bird with a yellow spot on each wing could guide a person to honey that wild bees had hidden in hollow trees. My mouth filled as I thought of the white honey, so sweet it made my tongue and lips almost sting. In the honey were pieces of wax that Mesfin and I chewed all day, long after the sweetness was gone.

"Ababba will never again be able to follow the honey bird," he said calmly. "But you and I could do it."

"Perhaps we could," I said. "When Emama returns from the market."

He went to a cow-horn hook and got down the gebeta board that Ababba had fashioned for us. Sometimes when we were out watching the goats, we would dig two rows of holes in the dirt and use pebbles to play the game, but now I was glad to run my hands on the wood of the board, knowing that Ababba's hands had been here.

For a long time we played, scooping up the seeds and dropping them into the holes in turn, capturing each other's seeds whenever we could. Suddenly, Mesfin spoke again. "Emama said she needed honey to make medicine. Would it be a good thing to have honey for her when she returns?"

"Yes," I said wistfully. How I wanted to do something to make up for breaking the pot yesterday. But my brother and I had been raised to obey and not bring shame to our relatives.

A shaft of sunlight fell through the door, making a small rock in the mud floor sparkle. "Look," I said. "Afternoon has come and the rains have not. Maybe the rainy season has already been milked dry."

"How great would be my joy. But the rains will probably come again tomorrow. And drive away the honey bird," Mesfin said.

Emama always said, "When the rooster crows, darkness comes no more. When Maskaram arrives, the rains come no more." In the coming month of

Maskaram, we would celebrate the first day of the new year, and, a few weeks later, we would have an even better celebration—a *Maskal* feast.

Ababba had told us that on the eve of Maskal, people in villages and cities lit torches and paraded from house to house. The next morning, everyone gathered around a huge bonfire, where soldiers made war-boasts and promised to save their masters from any kind of enemy. So when the rains were over, Ababba and the other soldiers knew it was time to go out to fight again.

"We should sit outside and see if today will be the first day with no rain," Mesfin said. "Only right in front of the house. No one can see us."

I thought about that. How good it would be to greet the sun for just a few moments. How could that hurt?

"We are both strong," Mesfin went on. "And I could protect you."

"Not from a zar spirit or some evil sent by a buda," I said.

He laughed. "Where is your faith? Won't your cross protect you from those?"

My fingers went to my neck. These words were something Ababba might have said to tease Emama. And now Mesfin was thinking in the same way. Yes, I would show him my faith.

Cautiously, I stepped outside and crouched under the shade of the overhanging roof.

Mesfin followed. He tossed a small pebble toward one of the chickens, and it ran over to peck hopefully at the pebble. We both laughed. "I wish it were already the feast day of Maskal," Mesfin said, "and time to put that chicken into the wat."

"Perhaps Emama will return leading a sheep," I said dreamily, "and put it into the wat tonight."

"Maybe she will bring another Silver Queen." Mesfin's eyes were suddenly dark and sad. "To replace the cross that the branches tore from my neck last year when I was walking through the trees with Ababba."

It bothered me to have Mesfin walking around without a cross. I touched my own cross on its blue cord. When Mesfin and I were very young, Ababba had brought home two silver coins and showed us the face of the queen of a faraway land on each one, the

seven pearls on her crown, and the small star on
her shoulder. The next time he went on one of his
journeys, he took the coins with him and returned
with something different. A silversmith had melted the
coins down, he explained, and turned them into silver
crosses. Ababba hung the crosses around our necks.

I did not like to see the worry in my brother's eyes.
"I wish she would bring a golden pin to put in my
hair," I said boldly.

That brought the laughter back to Mesfin's eyes.
"You are always such a dreamer," he said. Only the
Amhara royalty wore gold.

I rested my head against his arm. When we sat on
the platform for hours, keeping the animals away,
I told him things I had never said to anybody else.
How I looked at a cloud and saw the horses from
the paintings in Emama's book come to life. Or how,
before I slept, I remembered something the little girl
in the market had told me—that river snakes wrap
their tails around farmers' fences at night and stretch
their heads into the sky to feed on stars. He never
laughed at me then.

"Listen," Mesfin said suddenly.

He stood up and I stood beside him, my fingers curled tightly around my cross.

"There," he said. "It's the honey bird again. You know what Ababba always said about birdcalls."

I listened carefully and thought I heard the faint birdcall. Battles had been fought and surrendered, won or lost, based on the cries of birds. Ababba had told of times when an entire army was assembled only to melt away to nothing—the brave soldiers running through the trees—because the voice of a certain bird was heard from the left instead of the right.

"It's an omen," Mesfin said. "It would be wrong to ignore what the spirits are trying to tell us."

I thought about Emama coming home from the long journey I had caused her to make. I thought about how her face would look if she saw a gourd full of honey waiting for her. My stomach longed to make for her that kind of happiness. But how could I disobey?
"I need another sign," I said.

We watched and waited for some time in silence. Rain clouds did not fill the sky. The chickens scratched happily in the sunshine. The honey bird called again, but otherwise I heard nothing. Then my fingers gripped Mesfin's arm. Something had moved at the edge of the trees where Ababba had sometimes hunted or found mushrooms for us to eat.

I was about to pull Mesfin inside when an antelope bounded out from the trees. We shielded our eyes, trying to see it clearly as it ran across the path that led to the stream and disappeared into the high grass on the other side.

"There!" Mesfin said. "There's your sign."

This time I had to agree. Ababba had always said that an antelope running across the path was sure to bring a person success.

"Go inside and get a gourd," Mesfin told me.

I studied this brother of mine who had gotten so tall and confident in the last year. I remembered the way we'd beaten the fire last night, and pride rose in my throat. Emama did not know how strong we had become. Then I hesitated. "You do think there could be zars in the forest, don't you?" I asked.

"Well, yes. Of course. But these days, I don't think

they are around as much as Emama says. Haven't we lived here for many years with no troubles?" It comforted me to see his face so resolute. Though I was not used to thinking of him this way, I suddenly saw that he could indeed be my protector now that Ababba was gone.

I got the gourd and followed Mesfin down the hill, across the field, and toward the trees where we could now hear the honey bird well.

The mountain in the distance stood tall and green, rubbing its head against the sky. During the big rains, it often disappeared for weeks, wrapped in a cloak of fog. Sometimes when this happened, Emama and Ababba would argue about whether the mountain was still there at all. Perhaps a saint had come back to walk on the earth and had told the mountain, "Remove yourself," and it had uprooted itself and gone to a far country for a little while.

"I'm surprised the bird hasn't flown away," Mesfin said.

I was surprised, too. It must be quite a friendly one and ready to show us a big store of dripping sweetness.

I hurried after my brother into the trees.

We hadn't walked very far before we were in a green, warm world. Leaves danced and trembled over our heads. "Come in, come in," the branches seemed to be calling. They welcomed us the way Emama said that people should always invite strangers into their houses, because strangers were guests of God.

"So why must we hide if we see a stranger?" I once asked my brother.

"Because anyone who comes to an isolated place such as this one would surely be up to no good," Mesfin had said.

The honey bird sounded quite close now. It appeared to be waiting for us. I stopped and bowed back, respectfully, to the welcoming branches. *Thank you for taking us into your home.* I raised my hands with the joy of being alive.

Ahead of me, Mesfin cried out and bent to study his right foot. I took a step toward him. Was it a thorn? And then the trees around us seemed to suddenly crackle with noise.

"Run!" Mesfin shouted.

I turned to flee. Out of nowhere, hands grabbed me. I shrieked and twisted, trying to pull away from the hands. But the spirits—or whatever had been waiting among the trees—did not let go. The last thing the branches and leaves heard was the sound of my desperate screams.

5 Lion Creatures

I came up out of the deep pit of sleep with a moan already on my lips. "Emama," I whimpered softly. "I dreamed of lion beings that grabbed me out of the human world." The beings had pulled my shamma over my head so that I couldn't see. We had jostled and bounced for hours on their unearthly steeds, and everything inside and outside of me now hurt. But even as I opened my eyes, I knew it was not a dream.

The first thing I saw was one of the creatures a little way away, with its human face staring at me from under a bushy golden and black lion's mane. Where the thing's shoulders should be, I saw only lion's fur. I let out a loud, hopeless wail. And then, like a miracle, there was my brother, scrambling toward me.

"Ayezosh," he whispered. "I'll take care of you."

"How can you fight these half-man, half-lion creatures?" In spite of my despair, I clung to his hand and covered it with kisses. How good it would be to die with someone I knew beside me.

He frowned. "They are not lions, but soldiers wearing lion's fur. See? Here one comes close."

After a moment, I saw that Mesfin was right—it was a man. And although I shrank back, he did not leap on me and tear me to pieces. He knelt and held something out with both hands. "Take it," Mesfin urged.

When I still didn't reach out for the thing, Mesfin took it. "For the sake of your father," the man murmured. The words were Amharic, but his accent was strange to me.

Mesfin pulled the skin from this strange fruit, broke off a piece, and put it in my mouth. It was delicious. "See?" he said again.

"Why did he say that about . . . our father?"

"I'm not sure." Mesfin waited until I swallowed and then put the rest of the food into my mouth, as tenderly as a bird feeding its baby. "But they have been talking a little bit to me." He answered the questions in my eyes quickly. "No, they won't tell me why they've taken us or where we're going. They've spoken to me of Ababba, though."

I swallowed the last of the fruit, trying to imagine how these men with the strange voices would know my ababba.

"They do not know that Ababba is dead," he said. "Because he was a great warrior, they didn't dare come into the house to take us. Instead, they coaxed us into the forest."

"So the—"

"Yes, the honey bird call. That was one of them."

I thought about the sound I had heard by the stream, and I shuddered. What if they had gotten me without my brother?

"They set the fire, too. They were hoping we would run into the woods, and, in the confusion, they could seize us."

"I wish we *had* run into the woods," I said fiercely. "Then they would have taken Emama, too, and she would be with us."

"No." I heard the scolding in his voice and was ashamed. "You and I are young. I'm afraid Emama would not have survived."

Emama. By now, she had surely returned from the market and stepped into our house, only to find that her little spiders had disobeyed her and run off. I began to weep, rocking back and forth, clutching my own arms as if I could hold myself in a close embrace. Over and over, I made the mourning sounds that Emama and I had made after Ababba died.

Mesfin patted my arm and clicked softly with his tongue, the way Emama used to comfort us when we were little. "Our emama's spirit is strong," he whispered. "I think she knows more than we know about who these men might be. But we mustn't speak of Ababba's death to anyone. Surely as long as they think he is alive, they will leave her alone."

Just then, I heard a shout. When I looked up, I saw a mule clattering toward us. I stared in amazement at how beautifully the mule's saddle was decorated. It was made of wood, just like Ababba's saddle, and covered with goatskin. But it was the saddlecloth that I couldn't stop admiring. It hung down, with a hole for a stirrup—a stirrup only big enough for a man's big toe to fit through. Shiny bits of silver danced on the cloth, clinking with each step the mule took. Even more fascinating was that in the middle of the saddle-cloth, someone had captured the likeness of a man.

The likeness showed a man on a galloping white horse. A long spear in his hand was piercing a snake creature that crouched almost under the feet of the horse. His face, brave and powerful, looked straight at me with both eyes—as the faces of good people always did in paintings. I suddenly remembered him from Emama's precious book. This must be Saint Giorgis, king of all the saints, killing the dragon that was going to eat the helpless maiden, Berutawit. If only Saint Giorgis would come here now and save me!

The man on the mule reached down and motioned that I should stand up and give him my hand. "Hold on," Mesfin said, helping boost me up behind the man.

"Where will you be?" The words came sputtering out and then all my breath was taken away as the mule began to trot. I tried to turn and see where Mesfin was, but I began to bounce up and down and had to hold on with all my strength.

After a while, I saw that we were on a path or road that wound up a mountain. Far below, I caught a glimpse of glittering water. Was it Lake Dembya, which I had seen once so long ago?

"Holy Mariam," I whispered between clattering teeth, "help me." When the holy mother and Yosef and baby Yesus had to flee from their home in Israel and go to Egypt, they lived for some time on an island in Lake Dembya. Perhaps they had come this way. Emama said that when King Herod's soldiers came close and were about to capture the holy family, a tree hid them. The soldiers heard only the sounds of a donkey braying inside the tree. Would I recognize such a magical tree if I saw one?

We rode until all my bones and teeth had been shaken loose and my legs ached so that I thought I would never be able to walk again and would have to pull myself along using only my arms. Sometimes we went up. Sometimes we went down, into places so steep, I leaned back against the back of the saddle until I thought I would touch the mule with my back. At one point, the man in front of me on the mule began to call in a high voice, the sound of his shout loud and ringing. A voice from some far-off ridge answered. For a while, the air was full of the music of men hollering the echoing sounds to each other. Then there was silence again.

Eventually, the mule slowed to a walk. I twisted until I could see a mule a little way back. To my relief, I saw Mesfin riding behind the man on that mule.

From time to time, I saw small houses off in the distance, one alone or two or three clustered together. As I stared at the houses, I wiped my tears away with my shamma, thinking again and again of Emama coming home and finding us gone. We also passed small bands of people walking on the road, going up or coming down. A baby carried on the back of a girl about my own size wailed as our mule trotted by. The girl gave me a quick look and then stared at the ground. She looked hungry and worn.

On we went, with the jagged teeth of blue mountains sharp in the distance, past a giant tree spreading its huge arms, and past a place where the road dropped away on both sides and my breath stumbled in my throat to see the valleys far, far below. After we were safely on the other side, the man gave a grunt and the mule stopped. For a few moments, we just sat.

I wanted to look for Mesfin, but I could hardly move. I heard the clopping sounds of other hooves and soon another mule was there, nudging its furry side against our mule and scraping my leg. Then a third one jostled close.

"Look how poorly these mules behave," the man said. "They need to be following a horse. But these days we must save all the horses for parades and battles." The only thing my eyes wanted to see was my brother and, praise be to God, there he was, on the fourth mule that came trotting up. His animal wore a saddle blanket with a picture of men holding spears surrounding a lion.

"You." I looked down and saw that one of the

soldiers was showing me that I should climb down from the mule. I slipped off, and he held me while I staggered forward, trying to get my stiff legs to work.

He laughed a little. His hand was rough and hurt my thin arm, but I was glad that he was holding onto me because I was like a stumbling baby and could hardly stand. The ground was rough and rocky. When the soldier saw how I was struggling on the rocks, he motioned for me to sit under a thin tree. From his bag he pulled something shaped a little like a fish and handed it to me.

"What is it?" I turned it over. The bottom was flat.

"A leather worker made these *berebaso* for my brother, who is about to become a priest." I had to listen carefully to his words in his strange accent. "I was going to give them to him the next time I visited my family, but I give them to you instead. For the sake of your father."

I saw that he was holding another one in his hand. He showed me that I was supposed to put them on my feet, which surprised me. His own feet were as bare as mine, and I had never seen anyone wear such things, but they stuck to me as I stood up and took one cautious step. At

first, I stumbled on the rocks even more. But at least the
bottoms of my feet could not feel the sharpness of the
rocks. After we had walked for a little way, my feet
started to like these strange berebaso.

He guided me to a place where water ran out of the
rocks. We sat there, drinking water that we cupped in
our hands and eating pieces of coarse bread that the
men carried in their leather bags. I showed my new
footwear to Mesfin and he smiled with admiration.
No doubt my own face was stained with tears, but his
had the look of a bold boy on an adventure. "Have
you found out anything more?" I whispered.

"Yes." His voice was low and careful, but also full
of excitement. "They are taking us to Gondar. It is
another two days' ride."

Gondar. I clutched my brother's arm, amazed.
Sometimes when Ababba was plowing, he sang:

Beautiful from its beginnings,
Gondar, hope of the wretched,
And hope of the great.
Gondar without measure or bounds.

This song rang in my head in time with the mule's hooves as we clopped on and on. "Emama," I whispered. "Can you make your way to Gondar?"

The next time we stopped to rest and eat, we sat only a little way from the road. A group of children stood and watched us with wide, longing eyes. Once or twice, the soldiers yelled in another language and chased the children away, but they always crept back. Finally, the soldiers shrugged and gave up.

"What is that language the soldiers are speaking?" I whispered to Mesfin.

"I don't know," he whispered back.

"They're barbarians, aren't they? The kind Emama always warned us about. Do you think they eat—"

Mesfin hushed me, glancing at the men uneasily. "I know they're not Amhara. They tell me that they are Oromoo and that their chief is a very important person."

For a moment, I thought I would pull the berebaso off my feet, but such a gesture might make the soldiers angry—and had these not been given to me in kindness? But I couldn't make myself eat another bite of their bread. I held it out to one of the watching children, who ran over and took it from my hand. She knelt and touched her forehead to my feet. I smiled, feeling for one moment like some important person as she dashed back and divided the small piece with an even younger girl.

The words that danced on the edge of my tongue were the ones the soldiers kept saying to me: "For the sake of your father." These words seemed to be some kind of courtesy when a person gave gifts in this land. Was anyone ever going to explain to me what the strange saying meant? And what kind of monstrosity was Gondar if it was filled with hippopotamus-eaters and other barbarians? I wished I could ask Ababba why he wanted to sing the praises of such a place.

6 Escape

From then on, when the soldiers gave me bread or dried meat, I ate only a few bites, just enough to dull the sharpest of my stomach pains. I did not want to taste food contaminated by their hands. When they saw that I was not eating, one of them gave me a small leather bag—again saying "for the sake of your father"—and indicated that I should put what I didn't eat into the bag so that I could eat it when I was hungry.

For the next two days we traveled endlessly. The monstrous mountains that loomed all around us made me feel very small and afraid. Both nights, I cried until I fell asleep, full of choking sorrow to be so far from Emama. The soldiers always made a fire, and I curled close to it, trying to shut out their voices and their laughter. I covered my head with my shamma and used the edge of it for my tears. Emama was strong, but she was not strong enough to climb up these high mountains and down into the valleys and back up the steep slopes. Even the mules panted, their sides steaming with sweat.

Late the second night, I decided I could bear the pain no more. I had never made a plan by myself, but gradually an idea came to me. Moonlight could help me pick my way along the path we'd just followed. Though I didn't know all of the steps to get back to my home, I could at least start by going back downhill. I had a little hard bread and dried meat in my bag. When that ran out, I would stand and stare at someone who had food, the way the girl had done to me.

I rose and moved calmly into the bushes. The soldiers watched me go, but no one made a move. Was it not a natural thing for a girl to need to go into the bushes? Fear pounded inside of me, turning my chest into a drum, but I was determined. I could not even tell Mesfin, because how could two people slip away?

Once I reached the bushes, I simply kept going.
I moved as quietly as moonlight, touching this stone,
flitting to that branch. There. I could do it. I heard
nothing behind me. Emama and I would find
someplace new to live, someplace even farther
from Gondar, even more isolated, where these—

A shout split the darkness.

Running feet.

I started to run, too, panicked as any small *dik-dik*
that dodged along the path with Ababba dashing
after it.

Feet slammed the ground right behind me. Hands
grabbed my shoulders, my arms. I wept and wriggled.
I twisted and bit and tried to tear away from those
hands, but the soldiers were much stronger than I was.

When they had carried me back to the fire, one
soldier took a leather thong from his bag. He looked as
if he was ready to beat me, and I whimpered, covering
my head with my arms, but a second one said
something that stopped him.

"Wait," a third said in Amharic. "Let her brother
talk to her."

Mesfin wiped my eyes and said "Ayezosh" over and over. "You cannot put Emama's life in danger, even if you can get back there," he whispered. "Also, Emama would want you alive, not killed by these soldiers. She would want it more than life for her own self. Ayezosh. This is the time to be brave. This is the time to live."

I held onto his arm for a long time, thinking of Emama's face. Slowly, I came to accept it—he was right. She would insist that I go forward. It seemed years ago that I had sat in our house thinking that I wanted to see the glories of the world. I wished I had never had such a thought. *Holy Mariam, holy Saint Giorgis, help me be strong*, I said in my heart. Bit by bit, I must swallow my longings to be home and set my face toward Gondar instead. Could I do it? Emama would say that I could. "Come, child," she told me as she gave me each bigger pot, teaching me to carry the water. "Little by little, the egg will walk."

7 *The Giants' Compound*

As for Gondar, may God be praised that I had the words of Ababba's song to hold in my heart as we neared our destination. Gradually, we saw more and more people along the road until, finally, flocks of people walked and stood everywhere. I never knew there were so many people in all the wide, flat world.

The women were like butterflies in their gleaming gossamer dresses with the bright embroidery that Ababba had described. Others wore blue cloaks that glinted with gold. More soldiers stood along the road and shouted greetings to our soldiers. I stared at their shields, which were covered with soft, elegant cloth and trimmed in gold or silver. Three men trotted by on horses that were so dressed and decorated, I could hardly see any horseflesh or hair under all the finery.

As our mules clopped along, a band of music makers ran up, keeping pace with the animals. Two men and a woman were singing while, at the same time, another man was crying out comments that made people laugh or cheer. A fourth man, holding some kind of instrument, ran right alongside my mule, looking up at me. I wanted to shrink away from his gaze. What was he looking for? He was so intent on my face that he didn't notice a ditch of water and fell flat into it, sending up a splash of water and mud.

His companions laughed and shouted. I turned to see him pull himself out with a grin. He sang, "They have the look of one who walked these streets of old, one who was not afraid of spears or swords or cannons." He moved the bow across the string of his mud-spattered instrument. "Not like the one who is stuck to his house as burnt injera sticks to the griddle."

I was relieved to hear the words in Amharic, but what could his song mean? His voice drifted after us as we clattered up in front of the boundary marker that was wrapped around Gondar—not a fence made of thorn branches but a wall of one stone on top of another.

I sucked in my breath as I stared at the brown stones in the wall and the mountain of rocks I could see rubbing the sky beyond the wall. Never had I felt so small and ragged. "There are twelve gates," the man whose mule I shared told me with pride in his voice. "The Gate of the General, the Gate of the Musicians, the Gate of the Spinners—"

I heard a slap, and the mule with Mesfin on it suddenly pushed ahead of ours. "Ayezosh," Mesfin called as he passed. "When spiders unite, they can tie up a lion." A moment later, there we were, riding through what the soldier told me was the Gate of the Judges.

"Prepare yourself," the soldier added.

But nothing could have prepared me for the wonder that was Gondar. Hope of the wretched, indeed! Was there hope for *me* here? Only if Saint Giorgis would have pity on another helpless maiden.

As we moved slowly forward, my eyes tried to drink in everything. I realized that the stone mountains had doors in them and must in reality be huge houses. Apparently giants lived in this place. At least ten of these houses sat inside this compound surrounded by the thick wall. They had doorways and windows, but they were unlike any house I had ever seen before. Even the *wanza* trees were like tiny children, bowing before the great houses.

The deep growl of a beast from somewhere behind me made me gasp and clutch at the soldier. "Ayezosh," he said. "It is just the lions."

"Lions." I tried to say the word calmly, but my voice choked on it and came out as a squeak. I, the girl who thought I would never have to look upon a lion, was inside a compound with them.

"They are in their own house," the soldier reassured me. "How could an emperor not have lions? But they are quite tame."

An emperor? Before I had time to think about all these amazing words, the soldier pulled the mule to a stop, leaving me with my astonished thoughts. We were now directly in front of one of the stone houses. I gaped to see three doorways, so tall a regular person wouldn't have to stoop to enter them. Above those three, floating far too high for any person to walk

through, were three more curved doorways framed
in stones that made a pattern of brown and red.

"Come in." I was startled to see that a man in a
shining white shamma had come up beside the mule
while I was staring. So ordinary people must live safely
among the giants. Out the door of the house hurried
an old woman.

She motioned for the people who followed her to
hold up shammas on either side of our mule. "It's not
fitting for a lady to dismount in front of everyone's
eyes," she cried out.

Now the talk was of ladies? I looked around.
Then I realized the man had cupped his hands and
was indicating that I should step down into them.
"Welcome in the name of the *negusa negst*, the King of
Kings," he said. "Enter the castle built for an empress."

It was as if I had stopped thinking and stumbled
into a dream. When Ababba had spoken of Gondar,
why had he said nothing of castles? Or giants? Or
the King of Kings? Why was I here, and what kind of
sacrifice was I going to be? Where had Mesfin gone?

I looked around for him, but the old woman began

to call orders, and some younger women—one a girl about my size—tugged me through the door, up a strange stone path, and into a room. "My brother," I said weakly. "Where is—"

"Quickly," the old woman cried. "All her old, ugly clothes must be removed and new ones put on. You know Empress Menen would not want to see her this way."

So I was not to be a sacrifice but changed into a butterfly? My skin was washed and oiled. The smell of the oils made my head seem to float away. I could feel my aches from the mule ride melting, and, in spite of my worries, I began to relax as the women took over. After the rough, strange words of the soldiers, my own language sounded delicious to my ears. At least I was back among my own people again.

As if from a far distance, I watched myself being dressed in a dazzling white, soft dress with bright colors at the borders of it. A matching shamma was draped around my shoulders. They put the gold of royalty in my ears and a pin in my hair. I resisted only twice—when the women tried to take my cross and my new berebaso.

"We will bring you a much better cross," the old woman insisted. "One made of delicate gold just like the earrings."

"And dainty shoes for your feet," someone else told me, holding them out.

But I refused, dropping the shoes on the floor. I did not like the look of these. Wherever I was going, I had to stand strong. Best I wear something that someone had given me in kindness and that had carried me this far. As for the cross, I would rather have had my head chopped off entirely than let go of something so precious, something Ababba gave to me.

"Leave them," the old woman said. "No one will notice such simple things under her finery." As she spoke, she placed a strand of beads around my neck. I touched a bead with wonder and joy. Amber.

"Where is my brother?" I asked again. He had said he would take care of me. Sometimes when I was standing in the stream near my home, I would look down and see my own brown feet become wavery and lopsided, as if in a different world. Now, somehow, I had been pulled into that or some other strange, lopsided place.

"Listen to me, child," the old woman said. "Listen carefully. I'm sure you know nothing of the customs of the emperor's court."

I tried to listen, but the perfume of the oils was still making me dizzy.

"You are here because the emperor wishes it. Soon you will meet him. When you enter the room," the woman said, "you must sink to the floor by bending your right knee. Press your forehead to the floor at the entrance to the room."

I began to shake. What was she telling me? I couldn't concentrate. I would surely get it wrong.

"When you are halfway to the throne, press your forehead to the floor a second time. Do this a third time at the foot of the throne. And kiss the hem of the emperor's robe." She paused and looked at me with something like doubt or pity in her eyes. "If the emperor is pleased with you, he might hold out his hand to be kissed, instead of his hem."

I didn't ask what I wanted to ask because I didn't

dare question this woman with the authority in her voice. But *why* was she taking me to meet the emperor? What did the emperor want with me? "My brother," I whispered. "Where is he? I can't go to meet the emperor without my brother."

Was it my imagination that the women exchanged glances then? "Your brother will be with you," the old woman said. "Here, my child. You must show me that you understand how to approach the throne. And when you leave, you must walk backward. Never turn your back on the King of Kings."

I did it over and over until she was satisfied that I had it right. "Are you taking me there right now?" I asked.

The old woman laughed, but it was a harsh, grating sound. "I will not be the person to take you, child. And not now, of course. Emperor Yohannes is not listening to any petitions or greeting anyone this day. We will feed you and you will sleep here." She gestured with her chin at a bed across the room. "It may be two or three days before you go to the King of Kings."

Sleep here? In this big room without any animals or

my dear emama or brother?

"Throw these old clothes away," the old woman told one of the servants.

No. I clutched them to me, skittering away from the women across the floor of the room. In the middle of the floor lay a big piece of thick cloth covered with swirling designs and flowers. I walked carefully around it and went to the bed. It was made of wood and draped with decorated cloth. I placed my clothes and the leather bag that the soldiers had given me under the bed. When I turned, I saw that the women were all still standing, watching me.

Perhaps I was supposed to give them something for all their trouble. I went over to the shoes I had dropped on the floor, picked them up, and held them out to the girl. "Do you want these?"

The girl looked at the old woman, who bent and whispered something to her. Then the girl stepped toward me and held out both hands, shy but respectful. As I gave them to her I said, "For the sake of your father."

I could not have been more shocked at what

happened next. The girl dropped the shoes on the
floor and fled the room with an agonized cry. For a
moment, everyone stood in terrible silence. Then the
old woman pushed the others out and came back to
put a wrinkled hand on my arm. "I apologize for her
foolish behavior. She will learn to serve you well,
I promise."

"But . . ." My lip was quivering. How would I ever
learn what I needed to know in this place? "Isn't that
what you are supposed to say when you give a gift?
The soldiers said it to me."

"This girl has no father." Her voice was kinder than
before. "She thought you were insulting her." She
studied me carefully. "The soldiers were talking about
your father, child. *Your* father."

"Mine?" I stared at her stupidly. "What about my
father?"

"Your father was kin to some of the soldiers who
brought you here. And his father was a great warrior
and respected by all of them. But I see you know
nothing of this."

What? This could not be true. My father's father

had worn a headdress of lion skin? My own grandfather . . . an Oromoo? Speaking in a strange tongue?
Eating God only knows what? I stood in stunned
silence, thinking that perhaps next the earth would
open and swallow me in one slurping gulp.

8 In the Walking Dream

The old woman had pity on me then. "You need food more than talk," she said. "I will have something brought to your room."

"And my brother?" I managed to squeak out.

"Of course. His room is just on the other side of the castle. I will send for him."

While I waited, I studied the shamma they had placed on my shoulders. It was so light and delicate that it seemed to float. "Look," I told Mesfin as soon as he entered the room. "A fellow spider must have spun it. Have you ever seen anything so fine?"

He walked all the way around me, making admiring clicks, and then I walked all the way around him to see his new finery. What would Emama think?

We sat on polished wooden stools in front of an

exquisite flat basket. Servants poured water for us to wash our hands. Then they filled the basket with white injera. They carried in bowl after bowl of food, dipped their ladles in, and put heaping spoonfuls onto the injera. I counted ten different dishes, most of which I didn't even recognize. The *doro wat* dripped with thick pieces of chicken and large eggs. Even *one* of these dishes would have seemed sumptuous on one of the feast days with Emama and Ababba.

I bent and let the delicious smells come up into my head, torn between hunger and bewilderment. "What kind of strange web is this for two humble spiders to dangle from?" I asked Mesfin when we were finally left alone. I did not dare speak loudly. Who knew what servant ears might be nearby? "Do you think we will have to meet the giants who built these houses?"

For once, my brother looked puzzled and troubled. "I have a powerful feeling that I have been here before," he said slowly. "I do not remember any giants. I think these castles—as they call them—were built by human beings. Here's an amazing thing! The servants told me that our father's father was a great warrior."

"I know that."

"Oh." His anxious expression disappeared and he laughed at my bold words. "Well, how knowledgeable you have become. If information is given even to girls in this place, why should I worry? Let's eat."

I tore off a piece of injera. The rich oils made my tongue cry out for each different dish to be first. And I couldn't stop looking at us in our fine clothes. Ababba would have approved of this finery. But Emama—how worried she must be. If only there could be some way to let her know where we were.

Mesfin took a bite, and his sigh of satisfaction brought me back to the food and my brother's face. "Did the servants also tell you that our grandfather was a soldier for an emperor? He fought so bravely that a marriage was arranged for him with the emperor's youngest daughter."

I gaped at him. What kind of astonishing news was this? "Your ears must have deceived you," I said. "Our grandmother . . . the daughter of an emperor? How could that be?"

"Here's exactly what the servant said. 'In these

troubled times, there are four different kingdoms in Ethiopia with four different rulers. Your grandfather served His Majesty Tekle Giorgis II, the king over all of the other rulers.'" Mesfin spread his arms wide in a majestic gesture. "The King of Kings."

These proud words made me giggle. "And are you saying we have blood and bones of a King of Kings inside us? But . . . that's . . . glorious, isn't it?"

"Well, it is, except—" He pressed his lips together quickly. Someone must be approaching. I scooped up a fat piece of chicken in some injera and lifted it toward him, as we always did on the feast days. When he opened his mouth, I popped the big bite in. He rolled his eyes with the wonderful taste of it, and I had to giggle again to see him chewing such a large morsel.

This talk of emperors and warriors seemed no more real to me than one of Emama's stories. Wat and injera in my hand. My brother by my side. Those were the real things I must cling to.

"Rain and children give joy even when they annoy." It was the old woman, who had returned on quiet feet to stand beside my stool. She patted my brother's head and looked down at him fondly. "Eat and grow strong."

As we ate, Mesfin asked the old woman many things. My brother was a boy—almost a man—and no one thought ill when a boy-man asked questions. She told us she had been a servant for royal families in Gondar since her childhood. But whenever Mesfin asked what I was longing to hear about—our father's parents or our mother and father—she would gently speak of something else, in the way people did when turning talk from something that should not be discussed. What she had told me earlier was all she seemed willing to reveal.

But someone, sometime, must surely tell us more. For the first time in many days, I felt a flutter of joy. I now knew something more about my grandfather— my father's father. What if my very own father had once been a baby in this room? Here in this majestic city, surely I would finally learn more about what had happened to my father and my mother.

That night, I could not rest. The bed was too soft and the questions in my mind too urgent and puzzling. *Why? How? How? Why?* Finally, I climbed out of bed and lay on the cloth in the middle of the room, where I eventually fell asleep.

Oh, the things we learned those next two days as we stared from the windows of our castle. I discovered that, being of the royal family, even *I* could ask questions, and no one would scold me for being disrespectful. The castles in the compound had housed many different emperors. The huge one had been built first—about two hundred years ago—to be the home of Emperor Fasiladas. People called it Fasil Gemb, and the present King of Kings, Emperor Yohannes III, lived in Fasil Gemb with his empress, Menen.

The beautiful castle in which we sat had been built last, less than a hundred years ago, and was called the empress castle. I tried to imagine the empress who had dreamed of a building this wondrous and the workmen who had made the dream real.

Our castle sat with two others at the opposite end of the royal compound from Fasil Gemb. From my window,

I could see its high egg-shaped towers and a smaller castle beside it. A great open space lay in the middle.

As I gazed out, sudden roaring made me tremble like a goat in rainy season. I turned to the girl I had tried to give the shoes to. "What is it?"

"The servants are giving meat to the lions." She did not speak unless I spoke to her first. Then she was respectful but never friendly, no doubt because of my ugly mistake with the shoes. Something about her reminded me of the girl I had laughed with in the market long ago, and I wished I could see her smile.

The old woman sent the others on errands—"go here"; "do this." She was quick to tell me, "If you treat a servant as an equal, you make him into a ruler over you." She also told Mesfin and me that we were not to go outside the castle until the time came to present us to the King of Kings. So we had many hours in which to try to untangle the knots of what people had told us—and what they would not say.

We heard talk of powerful people. People spoke in hushed voices about General Ali Alula, the Oromoo chief of the soldiers who was the highest noble in the land, and the emperor's guardian. He lived in his own capital, Debre Tabor, a two-day mule ride from here.

Ababba, my Amhara grandfather, had been a palace guard—as had my Oromoo grandfather—in this compound long ago. "What else have you learned about our family?" I asked my brother. "What else did Emama keep from us?"

I saw his jaw quiver and knew that he was unhappy or angry. "People mostly lower their voices or shake their heads when I ask questions. Many around here appear to be afraid—even proven soldiers who have been in many battles."

We could make no progress in figuring out what had happened to our Oromoo grandfather and the princess he married, our grandmother. All Mesfin had learned was that Gondar had had thirteen different emperors since our grandmother's father sat on the throne.

"Thirteen?" I shook my head at him. Was this some kind of tale? "How can there have been enough time for thirteen rulers, since our own grandfathers served this King of Kings?"

"The tree of the people descended from King

Solomon and the Queen of Saba has become very wide, and many men can lay claim to the throne as their descendants." My brother leaned out the window as if his eyes could taste everything in the big courtyard. "Most of the ancient emperors had many children. Some had more than one family."

For just a moment, hearing the names of King Solomon and the Queen of Saba, I was back in our small house, listening to Emama's voice, feeling her fingers in my hair as she told me the story of Solomon and the ancient Ethiopian queen.

"Not only have there been thirteen emperors here in Gondar," Mesfin went on, "but kings from other branches of the great tree rule other Ethiopian kingdoms. These days bring frequent challenges to the King of Kings. I hear of much fighting."

I was tired of trying to follow these tangled threads. The only things I cared to know were what had happened to our father and mother and grandparents and why someone wanted my brother and me in Gondar. As Mesfin talked, my heart began to devise its own plan. If we were so important, we could surely find a way to ask the King of Kings to bring Emama here. Until then, I must store everything in my heart so that I could tell Emama of the many marvels.

Never had I been this warm, this well-fed—and this dazzled by magnificence. A whole world paraded under my window. I now saw that mules were determined, worried workers but that horses dashed and danced. Both Mesfin and I loved watching them prance in their beautiful decorations. One of the servants, pausing to see what had us so interested, said, "Oh yes, you are true Ethiopians. All Ethiopians love their horses."

She told us about an ancient emperor whose beautiful horse was captured and carried away to a distant land. In captivity, the horse would neither eat nor drink nor let anyone ride upon its back. A royal Ethiopian, also captive in that land, offered to tame him. As soon as the prince leaped on the horse's back, the horse and rider dashed away. The loyal horse did not stop until he had traveled across all the mountains of Ethiopia to Gondar, where he fell dead with exhaustion.

"After that," the servant said, "our emperors and generals began to take their war horses' names as part of their own. If the horse was named Suviel, the soldiers would call their leader Father of Suviel." I could tell from the look in my brother's eyes that he would be up on some horse's back himself as soon as we were allowed to leave this castle.

I discovered that the music makers I had seen on the first day were called *azmaris*. They walked among the castles singing songs of love and war, and playing the instrument called a *masinko*. Although sometimes they sang of a man's greatness, they could also mock and cut with their songs. They did not care who they scorned—the rich and the great, even a general, even an emperor.

This I learned from the girl I had insulted. She usually sat spinning in a corner and would come instantly whenever I needed something. I could tell she wished she didn't have to speak to me. "The woman singing now is my aunt," she replied when I asked her how she knew so much about the azmaris.

"Don't the rich and great ever become angry when the azmaris mock them?" I asked another servant.

"Long ago, when my mother's mother was a child," she replied, "some Gondar azmaris—about thirty in all—ridiculed powerful General Mikael. He grew full of wrath. They not only did not stop, but they began to mock his horse, which had run away during battle."

Remembering the great pride the rulers had in their horses, I drew back, afraid of what she would say next.

"General Mikael signaled to his soldiers, who fell upon the azmaris and tore them to pieces. Before the women could even scream, all the azmaris were dead except for one young man."

"What happened to him?" I cried out, hoping to hear that at least one had lived and perhaps gotten some revenge.

"He stumbled a little way toward the general, and then he fell dead without saying one word." She saw my horror and asked my pardon for upsetting me. "Several months after that," she assured me, "the general's horse twice threw him to the ground in just the place where the azmaris had died. My grandmother said all the people knew this to be an omen that General Mikael's power was lost to him forever."

This story filled me with dread and wonder. I wondered if it had something to do with Mesfin and me. After all, it was the Amhara way to hint at things but not say them directly. But what? What kind of danger were we in?

On the morning of the third day, the old servant woke me, crying out that the time had come to go before Emperor Yohannes III, the King of Kings. She hurried my brother and me to one of the downstairs halls and made us practice our parts again and again. She took my brother's shamma and showed him how to wrap it around his waist and cross it on his chest, with the ends up over his shoulders. This was called *megebgeb*, she told him, and he would wear his shamma this way only when he was in church and before the King of Kings.

On and on she talked, making me more and more afraid. All head coverings had to be removed in the emperor's presence. It would be terrible to turn one's back on the emperor. If the emperor stood, only the empress and the patriarchs of the church could remain seated. No one could walk behind the emperor. In ancient times, the emperor would sit behind a curtain with a veil over his face. Now he sat under an umbrella of red velvet, decorated with gold and jewels.

The old woman rushed us out of the castle, reminding me of one of our chickens that squawked and danced around her chicks, ready to peck me if I came too close. The bright light dazzled my eyes and I blinked. As if from a far distance, I heard the woman say something about an umbrella to shield me from the sun. A loud growl made me leap and shudder. "Ayezosh," she soothed. "It is only the house of lions."

Then, almost as if we had flapped on bird wings, we were inside the coolness of another castle. How we walked there, I cannot say. Nor did I notice anything around me except that we were in a great, bare room. Vaguely, I was aware of murmuring voices. The smell of hot peppers and roasting meat floated in the air, mixed with the sweet scent of some flower. Then I noticed the people in bright robes at the other end of the hall.

We walked together, my brother and I, bending low as the old servant had shown us. Without my brother, I think I would have fainted from fright. "Kiss the emperor's hem," the old servant had told us. "He may hold out his hand for you to kiss instead." He did not.

"Why have these children come before me?"

I did not look up, but I had been told the emperor did not speak for himself but through a man who was his mouthpiece.

"I have ordered it." At that cold, powerful woman's voice, I raised my eyes just the smallest bit and saw curling shoes with pearls on them. This must be the Empress Menen.

"Who are these children you have ordered to come before me?"

These were the questions no one yet had answered for Mesfin and me, though we had asked many times. I swallowed to clear my ears, trying to still the pounding in my neck and head so that I could hear the answer.

When it came, it could not have surprised me more. "They are the grandchildren of your sister, who died when you were imprisoned on Amba Wehni," the cold voice said. "I have not yet found their father, your sister's son, but my soldiers are searching for him."

At that, such a buzzing filled my ears that I heard nothing more except the sound of my own breathing. When I felt Mesfin nudge me, I gave a quick glance upward and saw that the woman was addressing me. "You will stay in the empress castle, to learn the things that befit your rank."

"And this boy who does megebgeb before me?" said the emperor's voice.

For what seemed a long time, Empress Menen did not say anything at all. Then she spoke to Mesfin in that frightening voice of hers. "We will find a place for you," she said. "For the sake of your father." In her mouth, the words sounded altogether different.

9 Angel Voices

Somehow I must have gotten out of the hall, touching my forehead to the floor at the appropriate places. I must not have turned my back upon the emperor, covered my head in his presence, sat while he was standing, or otherwise ruined myself—because I found myself back in my own room, alone and trembling but with my body still in one piece. The servants brought me sweet hot tea and honeyed cakes, but I could not eat and I could not stop shivering. I couldn't even remember most of what I had heard. Two things clung to me. My father was still alive. And I, Saba, was not only of the blood of Makeda, the mighty Queen of Saba, but I was related to the King of Kings now on the throne.

Over and over I tried to untangle the knot. My

grandfather had married a daughter of His Majesty
Emperor Tekle Giorgis II and had a son. This son
would be the man the soldiers were searching for—
my father. But my father was dead. If not, why had
Emama said he was?

I tried to approach the knot another way. My
brother had said there were thirteen different emperors
between Emperor Tekle Giorgis II and the current
emperor, who must be my great-uncle. Where were my
grandparents and my parents during the reigns of those
thirteen emperors? Why did my brother and I live with
our mother's parents, so far from Gondar? And why
had Emama and Ababba said nothing of all this?

These thoughts chased each other around and
around. After they had become very old thoughts, a
new one came. For the first time, it occurred to me to
also wonder whether my brother might be destined
to become the next emperor. "Where is my brother?"
I asked the servants. "I would like to see my brother."

They did not know where he was. Probably he had
been taken to one of the other castles, the old servant
told me. She would try to find out which one. In the

meantime, I must be brave.

How could I, a little spider alone in this big castle, be brave? The answer came to me immediately. I was a descendant of the Queen of Saba. Surely that was why my mother had given me the name Saba. How could I not be brave? But though I told myself these words, I could not stop shaking. If only my emama were here to soothe me and whisper "Ayezosh" in my ear. And my brother. He had promised to take care of me. Wherever he was, why didn't he send for me?

I slept fitfully that night and had not stopped trembling when the old woman came to my room early the next morning. She told me today was New Year's Day and I must go to church with the rest of the royal family. New Year's! Of course, it now must be the month of Maskaram. How long it seemed since I had stood at the stream thinking of just this day. Then, I had assumed I would welcome the new year with my emama, as I always had. Even in a frightening dream,

I would never have imagined this.

The old servant helped me dress. Carefully, she placed the beads of amber around my neck. "Are you sure you don't want to wear these beautiful shoes?" she coaxed.

I said nothing but put on my sturdy berebaso. They and the silver cross were my roots to the life I had before Gondar. "Will I see my brother in church?" I asked her.

"I will pray to God that you will."

When we went downstairs, three servants approached me, bowed, and put flowers into my hands. "*Melkam addis amet*," they told me. "Praise be that the new year has come." The old servant slipped me three silver coins, and I understood that I was to give one to each of the servants, along with my thanks.

This time when I went outside, there was no blinking in the sun because the servant girl immediately held a red umbrella over my head and stepped with me each step. I looked up at this small red sky and did not know what to think. Although the umbrella was beautiful and grand, everything that was happening to me was frightening, and I was desperate to see my brother.

The emperor and empress themselves walked far ahead of us, step-stepping to the beating of a huge drum. To my sorrow, I could not see a head that looked anything like my brother's. I shrank into myself, sad and afraid.

I had never been inside a church before and had only heard Emama's descriptions as she showed me her precious book on feast days. But all my feelings of strangeness fell away the moment I climbed the stone stairs, removed my shoes, and stepped into the church of Debre Birhan Selassie.

How many times had I asked for a miracle and no miracle happened? Now one did. As I gazed in awe at the ceiling, my trembling stopped. Angel after angel after angel looked down, catching my gaze in their own. I had not known that angels had such kind faces, with wings curling up around their cheeks. I had not known their eyes were so wide and warm with encouragement.

I dropped the flowers I had been clutching. It seemed to me I heard the angels' voices. *Was not the holy Mariam a simple girl when the angel appeared to tell her that Yesus Cristo would be born to her?* That is what I thought I heard the angels saying to me. *Did not the angel tell Mariam "blessed are you among women"? You, Saba, have also been blessed. Take heart. Be strong.*

In that round church, I listened to the ancient language of *Ge'ez* for the first time. I heard low chanting and the soft thrumming of the priests using the palms of their hands on the drums. I saw their stately dance and smelled the incense that filled Debre Birhan Selassie with a sweet and pungent mist. Above it all, I seemed to feel the fluttering feathers of those hundreds of angel wings.

We stood through the whole service. When it was over and I turned to go, a priest stopped me. I kissed his cross, as I had seen others do, and he whispered a blessing to me. Slowly, I walked out among the lovely, dark juniper trees with their spicy smell. Beyond them, sun poured down like rippling gold. Pink, red, and orange flowers sprayed out of the earth and tumbled over walls.

I thought of the angel voices. Why should I be afraid? No one had made any move to hurt me. To the contrary, they had fed me well and put wondrous clothes and jewelry on me. I must remember holy Mariam, that other peasant girl who was startled out of her old life. If she could have courage, perhaps I could too.

As I walked home, I felt as if I had one foot in another world. It was the first day of the week— Wednesday, the day Yesus Cristo was born. It was the first day of a new year. And I was a blessed new Saba.

10 *Hope of the Great*

After I heard the angel voices, the whole world seemed wonderful and new. I was in beautiful Gondar and, although I hadn't seen my brother since that fearful day with the emperor, I knew that he was somewhere close by. Also, I had created a good plan. What was to prevent my asking, once I had a chance to approach my great-uncle, the King of Kings, for Emama to be brought to Gondar?

I was now free to move around, so I spent the next day outside, with the girl holding the red umbrella over me. Skittish as a mule facing a swift-flowing stream, I crept as close as I dared to the house of the lions. Though they were behind strong bars, I could not stop shaking as I stared at their swiftly padding, clawed feet and their swishing tails. The smell of old

meat and blood was more than I could bear. I hurried
away to study the castles and the other buildings.

Our house in the countryside was made from clay
mixed with straw. The roof was made of grasses caught
together at the top and hanging down low over the
sides. Here, every building I saw was made from rock.
Some of the castles had little round houses floating
high in the air, but even those were made of stone.

Now that I was not so dazzled by everything, I saw
that many of the castles had places where towers had
tumbled or rocks had slumped into heaps. I wandered
into one and saw that it was full of books, but it had a
musty smell that made me want to run out. In another,
a rat ran by my foot, making the girl and me scream at
the same time. Although our voices mingled together,

I had given up trying to talk with her. "I think we will stay outside" was all I said.

At home, we made or built or grew things for ourselves. Here, the compound bustled with people bringing in whatever was needed—wood for the fires, meat for the meals, shields and harnesses, jars and cloth. A number of small houses were used for cooking food. Servants rushed into them and delicious smells drifted out of them. I saw trees and gardens where someday Emama, Mesfin, and I could walk and talk for hours.

The empress castle where I stayed was near the Gate of the Pigeons. For a long time, I stood and listened to the sounds the pigeons made as they chuckled and cooed in their house. I stayed far away from the house of the lions, with its smell of death. It made me cringe to watch those powerful tawny beasts that rippled constantly from one end of the cage to the other.

Which castle was my brother in? Was he seeing the same things I was? I longed to talk to him. Perhaps by tomorrow the old servant would know where they had taken him.

But when she came to my room the next morning, the only thing the old servant said was, "God be praised—you have found favor with the priests. They have invited you to receive instruction from one of the teaching priests."

I thought about the loneliness that sat heavy on my shoulders this morning. What I wanted most of all was to see my brother. Still, it would be good to have someone—anyone—I could talk with. "I think this is a good thing, is it not?" I asked.

"Oh yes. An excellent thing. A poor family would not be able to send their girl child to be educated, but you are a lady, and the jewel of education will be placed in your hands."

"Will my brother be taught with me?" I asked.

"Not with you," the old servant said. So he must have his own teacher.

The priest who came to teach me that morning wore a turban wrapped around his head. Under that, his lively face and eyes reminded me of the angels' eyes in his church. He sat quietly with his flywhisk, then began to ask me questions. Did I know my psalms? Did I know the 231 characters of the alphabet?

To both of these, I had to say I did not.

Could I tell him the story of Solomon and the Queen of Saba?

Yes! That I could. When I finished, he said, "*Melkam*," a word of praise. The story had other versions, he told me, but all agreed on the important points. For example, all agreed that King Solomon and the Queen of Saba had a son. After this son of Solomon had grown to be a young man, he went to Israel to learn from his father. When it came time for him to return to Ethiopia, he could not bear to leave the blessed Ark of the Covenant that held the tablets God had given to Moses with ten commandments for the children of Israel. "He brought the ark to Ethiopia," he said. "Did you know this?"

I said that I did, and he was pleased.

"Now my pupil may ask me a question," he said.

"How many angels are there on the ceiling of the

church?" I said quickly.

He smiled at that. "Ah, the artist painted so many that no one has ever been able to count. He did this in order to remind us that there are countless angels. Now perhaps we have had enough lessons for this day."

"May I ask you one more thing?" I knew it would be impolite to ask an elder something direct, but I had to start to harvest some small grains of information. He looked at me carefully, and before I could lose my courage, I said, "I think perhaps my grandparents died imprisoned on Amba Wehni. Can you tell me what kind of place that is?"

He brushed the flywhisk slowly back and forth. I liked to watch the long white hairs, which must have come from a horse or perhaps from one of the monkeys with long black and white tails. Finally he said, "I think you should know your country's history. In ancient times, the male relatives of an emperor were traditionally imprisoned on a flat-topped mountain called an *amba*. Some emperors made sure their relatives were well cared for. Others were not as careful."

I held my breath, hoping he would go on.

"The practice has fallen out of use in these times," he said. "But our emperor Yohannes III, King of Kings, spent a few years imprisoned on Amba Wehni. His sister, your grandmother, chose to join him there with her husband—and the chronicles say they both died there."

"And the woman who stood beside the emperor and from whose lips I heard the name of Amba Wehni? Who is she?" I wanted to hear what he would say about the empress.

I knew I had asked a second thing, and I would not have been surprised if he had not answered at all. Finally he said, "I will start your history lessons with an emperor who was brought down from Amba Wehni and crowned about a hundred years ago. He was called 'the severe one' by his people and was much beloved because the land was calm under his rule. Once, with the help of his sister, he had almost escaped from Amba Wehni wearing a disguise. Now, he wandered about the countryside in old and tattered clothes. Why do you think he did this?"

"So he could find out who his enemies were," I said promptly.

"Yes, and—even more courageously—what his subjects truly thought of his rule. One day, he saw an old man throwing sticks, as a means of divining the future, into a pond of water."

I knew that much wisdom could be held in stories. I drew up my knees, trying to catch each word and hold it in my heart. "The emperor asked what the sticks were saying," my teacher went on. "Because of the disguise, the old man assumed he was speaking to a peasant. 'The sticks say that the emperor will have a son,' he said. 'But they also say Wallata Giorgis, no descendant of the emperor, will govern the kingdom after the emperor's death.'"

My teacher was a good storyteller, and as I listened to his words, I could almost see the emperor hurrying home, taking off his tattered clothes, and ordering the death of anyone named Wallata Giorgis. One day, the empress bore a son to him, and he remembered the sticks. When he told her about the prophecy, she laughed. Then she said, "This Wallata Giorgis is even now in the palace with you."

My teacher's lips curled in a tiny smile. "The emperor leaped to his feet. 'Sit down,' said his wife. 'My name by baptism is Wallata Giorgis, and if you die when our son is young, I will govern, although I am not your descendant.'" My teacher flapped his flywhisk thoughtfully.

I bit my lip so I wouldn't cry out, "But what has this to do with the question I asked?" Instead, I waited, praying for patience—and answers.

"So Wallata Giorgis was two people," he eventually said. "In the same way, the woman you ask about is also two people. She is the Empress Menen, who ordered that Yohannes III be brought down from AmbaWehni so she could marry him. She is also the mother of General Ali and the widow of General Ali's father."

What strangeness was this? My stomach was hungry to hear whether this thing he called "history" could teach me of my mother and father. *Tell me more*, I silently begged. I would memorize each of my teacher's words and examine them later.

As if he had heard my thoughts, my teacher told me

about an earlier time when the disguised emperor of long ago gave his shamma to an Oromoo peasant for the man to wash. Then, as a test, the emperor began to say rude things about those in power. The peasant threw the emperor's shamma back to him, saying, "I was washing your cloak as a kindness to a poor man. Wash your own shamma. That will give you less time to criticize your superiors." My teacher paused. "Do you think the emperor liked this speech?"

"No," I said. "You said he was a severe man, and I believe it made such an emperor angry."

My teacher smiled. "You are wrong. When the emperor returned home, he summoned the man to Gondar and made him one of his most trusted servants. Thus the Oromoo people came to the court of Gondar and have been here ever since. Soon after that, the disguised and wandering emperor became sick with a fever. A kind young country woman brought him back to health."

"And he summoned the country woman to Gondar," I said, "and made her another of his most trusted servants."

I thought he might scold me for being impertinent, but he said, "I see you have a quick wit and tongue. In fact, he made her his wife. You are living in her palace. Just to show that the old man with the sticks was right, when the severe emperor died, his son was still only a child, so this wife, whose baptismal name was Wallata Giorgis, did indeed rule Gondar for many years."

I looked around. I was living in the castle of one who had grown up in the countryside far from Gondar, as had I. This thought gave me courage. If she could make Gondar her own, perhaps I could, too.

My teacher rose to go, and I hurried to say the words of farewell the old servant had taught me. "May God make thy words heard and cause thee to be ever green, like the juniper. May God make thee as broad as a fig tree and cause thee to shine like the moon."

"Amen," the priest said. I thought he was very pleased.

11 *Needles and Cloves, Dates and Silks*

Although my teacher—just as everybody else—would not speak to me directly of my family, the next day he told me enough of Gondar history for me to begin to understand a few of the things I was hungry to know. I learned that my grandmother's father, Emperor Tekle Giorgis II, spent his whole life in a struggle for the throne. He was knocked from his throne six times.

When he was deposed for the final time, the throne did not go to his son but was given to one of those thirteen emperors my brother had told me about. In fact, Tekle Giorgis's son—my great-uncle—hadn't been crowned until six years ago. My teacher made me see just how shaky power was in these times.

My stomach felt as if I had swallowed cotton thread as I tried to sort out this tangled knot. One thing was clear. Through birth, one could sometimes *become* the King of Kings, but it was not a simple thing to *stay* the King of Kings. I felt sure that my teacher was trying to tell me that these struggles for the throne were the reason why Mesfin and I had been brought here. All the rest of the day, I tried to puzzle it out.

The next day, I discovered that my teacher held many numbers and years in the palm of his hand. The most interesting one for me was the date when my grandmother was born, during her father's fifth reign. He also knew the day she gave birth to a son. I held my breath, listening. Though her father was in exile by then, great rejoicing secretly filled the land because this boy was the son of a princess and a popular warrior.

That boy was my father. My teacher began to write with a reed pen and ink on a piece of parchment as he talked. "When this boy grew to be a man, he was married to the daughter of one of the Amhara palace guards. Soon his wife had a son and, quickly after that, a daughter."

That would be Mesfin and me. I watched, transfixed,

as he dipped the pen again into the ink. He smiled at me as he wrote. "You see here the date of the daughter's birth."

I touched the dried black marks reverently and counted in my mind. So my age would be twelve years. It was a very interesting thing to know.

"Around this time," my teacher went on, "people began to murmur that their emperor was no stronger than a cut flower held by a child. There was much talk of a prophecy. According to this prophecy, a great emperor would be raised up, strong enough to overcome his enemies and truly become King of Kings over all Ethiopia. Some wise men said that a child recently born would become that emperor."

He paused. Did I want to hear what was coming next? I felt as though I could choke on my own breath. "This talk made danger for all royal children," he said. "Many of them suddenly disappeared."

I forced myself not to gasp. People must have thought my brother and I had been killed. But actually we had been hidden with Emama and Ababba, my mother's father and mother, all this time. A great tenderness for my mother and father filled me. Though I could not remember them at all, they must have been wise and brave to come up with such a plan and save our lives.

The knot in my mind suddenly untangled a bit. My great-uncle was not a young man. His empress was not a young woman. They must want either my father, if he was truly alive, or my brother to take over the throne next. I was filled with joy at my own cleverness. Now I could guess where Mesfin was. He must be studying even harder than I was. Amazing! He would someday rule Ethiopia.

I said my good-bye to my teacher with a smile on my face. The first thing Mesfin would surely do, when that glorious day came, was to bring Emama to Gondar.

The old servant was pleased to have my teacher coming to the castle. "He has so much goodness," she said, "that any winged devils will fly out of the rooms when he walks through them." When I was not studying, she added, I should lie on the bed and give orders to the servants. "Or spin. These are things a lady should do."

Gondar was known for its beautiful cloth, and the servants who lived in the empress castle spent much of their time spinning thread. After young girls cleaned the raw cotton, the other servants filled spindle after spindle with spun cotton to go to the weavers. But I did not want to give orders, lie on my bed, or sit and spin. Not when there was so much to see, and I was finally allowed to go out of the royal compound.

Now that I had figured out what my brother was doing, I wanted to see the city of Gondar. Each time I went out, the girl held an umbrella over me and a soldier or two stayed close beside me. Other servants came to carry whatever I needed or just to walk behind. If I even tried to pick something up, they hurried to take it from me.

Every day for two weeks, whenever I wasn't studying with my teacher, we climbed over one of the seven rainbow-shaped bridges that connected the royal compound with the city. If I wanted to ride a mule instead, the servants held a shamma so I could get on.

Then out the southern gates we would go, the servants walking beside and behind me.

It made me laugh to remember that I had longed to go to the village market with Emama. What would that market have? Perhaps some peppers and pottery and a bit of iron. Here, caravans with donkeys, mules, and camels streamed into the city each week loaded with goods. And such goods!

I saw things I knew—honey, wax, butter, horses— and also things I had never known existed—bottles and beads, needles and cloves, dates and silks. For the first time, I held a mirror in my hand and looked upon my own face. So that was what my ears looked like with their delicate gold earrings. And the plaits in my hair. Such a strange and magical thing to be able to see myself.

Every day, I saw Oromoo soldiers and nobles. Now it was obvious to me that Emama was just wrong, with her fear of the Oromoo and others she called barbarians. Why had she said such things when she knew my other grandfather was Oromoo? Perhaps she chose to forget my Oromoo blood because she didn't want it to be true. Or perhaps she wanted to ignore what she must have seen as the dangerous side of my family.

By now I had also learned of other Ethiopians who were neither Amhara nor Oromoo. The Tigray had a kingdom to the north of Gondar. Muslims lived in their own section of Gondar called Eslam Bet, the House of Islam, near where two rivers met. The servants told me that many of the Muslim men were weavers—perhaps the weavers Ababba had told me about—and they also made tents for soldiers. Others were traders.

Ethiopian Jews lived a little way outside the city. The women made glossy black pots, like the ones I had carried on my back when I took water from the stream. Many of the men worked as builders of castles and churches. Some were weavers. Others were blacksmiths and knew the frightening ancient magic of shaping iron and other metals. The servants and I quickly turned away if we ever heard the whooshing sound of the bellows or the clanging hammering of metal pieces. Everyone agreed with Emama that such people were likely budas.

It was also dangerous—though more tempting—to watch the men who worked with silver and gold. But I liked to see the way their fingers shaped a clay mold around a core of wax. First they heated the mold so the melted wax would pour out. Then they poured the gold into the mold, creating magnificent crosses for the priests to carry and pieces that would sit on the tables of the rich. As I watched, I ached. I would give up every beautiful new thing I had if only I could be back, standing beside Mesfin, smiling up as Ababba put my simple cross around my neck.

Meanwhile, my lessons continued. My teacher showed me manuscripts so that my eyes would drink in the shapes of the ancient letters. My finger moved from left to right on the page, tracing the flow of the letters while he read aloud. I could now recognize the shape of "b" on a parchment. But which of the seven forms of "b" was it? "Be, bu, bee, bah, bay, bi, bo," I chanted obediently as my teacher used a stick to touch each one in turn.

He was sometimes impatient and scolded me, calling

out, "What did I tell you just yesterday?" But other days he was gentle, as on the day when he showed me how to write my name. The fourth form *s* with the *ah* mark attached to its leg. The fourth form *b* with the *ah* mark also fastened to its leg. Together, the two letters said "Saba." Me.

One day during my history lesson, I told him, "It is very hard to learn about things that happened so long ago." I shook my head, rubbing my fingers together with the confusion. "All these names and dates. What would make them stick to a person? Perhaps only if a person knew he might be poisoned by a descendant of one of these emperors." I gave a brief smile. "For someone like my brother, I suppose these names come more easily, as he prepares to be King of Kings."

When I said this, my teacher did not speak sharply to me the way he sometimes did if he thought I was being lazy. He did not again tell me the story of Saint Yared, who learned to write music from watching a caterpillar climb and fall, climb and fall, climb and fall . . . and climb again. Instead, he tapped his flywhisk thoughtfully on the floor. Then he said, "Listen carefully to this story, and do not speak to me when I am finished, but only let my story move in your stomach until it turns into the bread of wisdom."

I leaned forward eagerly because I had learned that he always told stories for a purpose.

"Three boys were traveling in the forest," he said, "when a hyena leaped into their path. The boys, knowing that hyenas usually work at night, were frightened by this big, menacing one threatening them in the middle of the day. 'Whose protection are you under?' the hyena asked them."

Since the hyena spoke in the words of men, I thought perhaps the hyena was actually a buda, a man in the shape of a hyena. Perhaps not. Sometimes in stories, animals did speak in human tongue. But I did not interrupt my teacher to ask.

He went on, "The first boy said, 'I am under the protection of God, the great protector.'

"The second boy said, 'I am under the protection of the earth.'

"The third boy shook with fear. This hyena was clearly very powerful and very dangerous. He knelt down before the hyena and said, 'I am under your protection, O mighty one.'"

My teacher paused and gave me a long look. I thought he might ask my opinion of these answers, but after a few moments he simply went on with the story.

"The hyena turned to the first boy. 'You are protected by God,' he said. 'If I were to eat you, God would surely be angry with me through all eternity, so I will not eat you.'

"To the second boy he said, 'You are protected by the earth. If I were to eat you, I would have trouble finding any place where I could sleep and hide. Therefore, I will not eat you.'

"Then the hyena looked thoughtfully at the third boy. 'Ah . . .' he said. 'You are under my protection. That's good. Come inside my stomach and I will protect you fully.' And he ate the boy."

I frowned, waiting for him to tell me what the story meant, but he only rose and prepared to go. As I said my words of farewell, I hoped for my stomach to make wise bread quickly.

12 *At the Top of Fasil Gemb*

When my teacher was gone, I wandered from one
end of my room to the other and then back again.
I suddenly felt as caged as those lions in their house.
I had to get out. As I reached the door, the girl appeared
with my umbrella, but I waved her away and told her
I would only be in the shade and inside buildings. I did
not want a throng of people around me—or even one
other person—while I tried to untangle this new knot.

My teacher's words spun around and around while I
walked, but what did they mean? I was tired of trying to
figure out all of these complicated things by myself. In
Emama's stories, there was usually some kind of lesson
at the end. What would she say if she were here and I
could ask her how to figure out the lesson to this story?

She would probably say that it is when spiders unite

that they can tie up the lion. But, except for my teacher, I had no other spiders. I knelt and smelled a red flower. Where was my brother, and why was he too busy to call me to his side?

I closed my eyes, trying to think. Gradually, I became aware that the compound was humming with people. I looked up. The azmaris were standing nearby. The one holding the fiddle beckoned me over, and I saw that he had a tiny doll dressed as a soldier, with a spear and shield.

As I watched, he pushed a pointed stick into the ground and attached the doll to it. Then the musician lifted his curved bow and began to move the horsehair up and down the string of the fiddle. To my delight, the doll began to dance. I laughed and moved closer, until

I could see the string that went from the doll to the fiddler's bow.

Suddenly, the compound exploded with sound, the high *li-li-li* of women's joy cries. As we all watched, in rode a man on a horse with a whole crowd of soldiers behind. "General Ali comes to Gondar," one of the musicians sang, "to hold up the King of Kings."

The general was dressed simply, not in the glittering robe of an emperor. His face was calm and impassive. But something about the way he held his shoulders made me know that he was a man used to giving orders and having them obeyed. He stopped in front of Fasil Gemb, dismounted, and went up the stairs.

My gaze followed him as he entered the castle. My teacher had said that the severe emperor's son had spent much time decorating Fasil Gemb. He had employed Greeks and Ethiopians to decorate one room in ivory, topped by three rows of mirrors, framed in copper and gold from the faraway city of Venice, Italy. Pieces of painted cane turned the ceiling into a mosaic of colors, he'd said.

According to my teacher, another room had plates

of ivory with stars of all colors painted onto them. The emperor himself had joined in the work, exulting in the way his hand could produce a star as fine as any made by the Greeks. Many of the decorations were ruined now and the mirrors smashed. Yet the castle was still very elegant.

Ah! Why had I not seen it before? My brother must surely be instructed in *this* castle, the grandest of them all. I listened to one of the azmaris making up new poetry to be set to song. But I could not keep my gaze from the castle. Was Mesfin there? Well, I was the sister of a future emperor. What would anyone do to me? Taking a deep breath, I turned and walked purposefully up the steps of Fasil Gemb, my steps much stronger than my heart felt.

A guard looked up as I marched through the door, but he did not stop me. Other guards stood in the halls, but nobody spoke to me or held up a hand to show I should not continue. I glanced into the big room where Mesfin and I had gone before the emperor. It was empty now, except for the couch where the emperor had sat. I could see beautiful ivory and pearls in patterns on the couch, but between the swirls of the magnificent cloth, cotton poked out. In Gondar, nothing was as grand as it had once been.

I walked on. Some of the rooms had velvet hangings on the walls, or the tusks of some great animal, or glistening black pottery. Others were bleak and empty.

When my brother and I came to live here, I would order that the rooms once again be made beautiful, with mirrors and stars. I could feel my breath coming faster and faster as I looked around, sure I would at any moment catch some sign that Mesfin had been in these rooms. Perhaps God would give me great fortune and I would even see my beloved brother's face looking up, pleased and startled, from his work with his teacher.

But though I went from room to room to room, I did not see anything to tell me that he was or had been in this place. I found myself climbing a staircase and soon was frighteningly high, in the birds' domain, and staring out at the immense landscape.

From this perch, I could see across the trees that crowded the castle. Beyond the trees were the mountains. I wasn't sure from which direction Mesfin and I had come with the soldiers, but I tasted tears as I looked at the way the mountain ranges stretched back, back, until the last line was only a faint blue. I knew that these mountains gave Gondar safety from enemies. But they also stood between Emama and me.

What was Emama doing right now? How had she managed to plant the crops? I comforted myself, realizing that without Mesfin and me to protect and hide, she was surely not by herself but had moved into the village, where she could go to the market every week.

"I know we will come home to you soon, Emama," I whispered. "Or Mesfin and I will find a way to bring you here. I promise."

A movement caught my eye. Peering carefully down, I saw that three people walked in the garden far below me. One was Emperor Yohannes III, King of Kings. The second? That was easy. It was his wife, the empress with two identities. They both wore rich robes. The third was General Ali. Guards stood respectfully at a distance. Though the people were much too far away for me to hear their words, I studied the gestures of their arms and the way they stood.

I was high above them, but I could read their motions as clearly as the letters I was learning. These were three powerful people, and they were unhappy with each other. In fact, they appeared almost angry. A slight sound of loud voices reached me where I stood looking down.

At any moment, I was sure I would see my brother slip out of the castle and join them. Mesfin might be still a child in their eyes, but he had his own power. Perhaps it was not as much as if our ancestor had been a brother to Emperor Yohannes III rather than a sister, but clearly our grandmother and her warrior husband were much loved, and Mesfin, their grandson, would easily win the people's hearts in these discontented times.

But though I waited with hope in my eyes, my brother never came out. Instead, the three angry people in the garden scattered in three different directions. With their clothes huffing and settling around them, they reminded me of the hens that I had pushed from their nests in search of eggs.

I sighed and started carefully down the stairs. "Boys and smoke both disappear," my emama had said, "and no one knows where they go." How true her words had become here in the city of Gondar.

13 *The Hyena's Foot*

I intended to start searching the other buildings,
taking one upon me each day, but my plan was inter-
rupted by the arrival of Maskal, the celebration of the
finding of the true cross. It had now been seventeen
days since New Year's. The evening before Maskal,
I stayed up late, standing at the window to watch
people running through the many streets of Gondar,
carrying torches bright as tiny suns. An immense
sadness washed over me. Ababba must have lived
in this very city and seen these torches. He had left
this to protect my brother and me.

The next morning, the old servant rushed into my
room, calling out orders. The whole royal family was
to go together to the bath of Fasiladas, where there was
another castle, a pool used for baptisms, and a big

space for celebrations.

"Where is it?" I asked.

"Not far. Dress her!" she cried out to the other servants. "Make her beautiful to look upon."

My stomach leaped with excitement. The whole royal family, she had said. I prayed my brother would not be placed too far from me. How pleased he would be with all I was learning.

I stood still while they oiled me and dressed me in a gown. Always the gleaming white of the soft cotton. Always the beautiful embroidery of the borders, matched by the shamma. Today, they gave me gold anklets and placed a second string of beads around my neck. Red amber, truly as glorious as a rising or setting sun, just as Ababba had said. The old woman herself plaited my hair, and I smiled because her fingers reminded me of my emama.

I could feel my very bones inside of me singing a song of joy. What would Mesfin think when he saw me?

The old servant put a red velvet cloak around my shoulders. "You must wear these slippers," she pleaded breathlessly. "They'll have my life if you don't look your best today." And for the sake of my emama and my respect for all who had lived a long time, I agreed to slip off the berebaso that had become beloved to me and put on the awkward slippers with their pearls.

She instructed the other servants to dab kohl around my eyes, to emphasize their big, beautiful darkness, and to paint my hands with red dye. Then she hurried off. When she returned, I could see that she was pleased.

"It has all been done well," she said. "You make me think of a village girl whose father has decided it is time for her to be married. She sits at the door of her house spinning or cleaning corn so everyone can behold her. Yes, you will do." She gave a satisfied nod, and off she rushed again.

Wait, I wanted to call after her. *Stop. You must come*

back immediately and tell me more about this. But my tongue was not trained to give orders. I ended up meekly trotting down the stairs behind another servant.

My stomach whirled with what she had said. Marriage! I tried to remember Emama's exact words when we had been grinding grain back in our house. Those times now seemed so far away. If I was, indeed, twelve years old, I supposed that I was approaching the age of marriage. But as Emama had said, I was small. And why would they bring me here only to marry me off?

My brother would be able to explain it all to me. As we walked, great drums began to pound in salute to the emperor, and my heart leaped in anticipation and anxiety with every beat.

I searched the crowd for Mesfin's face. "What will happen when we reach Fasiladas's bath?" I asked one of the servants.

"Now that the rainy season has been milked dry and the rivers have stopped rushing and tumbling, it is time for the soldiers to begin their fighting season," she replied. "All the soldiers will parade before the emperor." She pointed her chin to a small, round building. "The soulless horse I told you about was buried there after he died."

"Why do you call him soulless?"

"He had great courage. Having no soul, he was not afraid to die."

A sudden thunderous crashing drowned out even the drums and battered my ears. Only the calmness of the servants around me kept me from throwing myself to the ground and covering my head with my arms. "It's just the soldiers firing their guns," a servant said. "The Maskal festivities have begun."

Perhaps everyone else in Gondar had a happy Maskal. Mine was spent in misery, standing with the rest of the royal family, watching as thousands of soldiers paraded before the emperor, his empress, and General Ali. The soldiers were a wondrous sight in their capes made of leopard and lion skins, their lion headdresses, and their shields, but after the first few hundred, even such glories began to seem commonplace. I only wanted the wondrous sight of my brother's face.

Next came the great chiefs, bringing their tribute—honey, butter, cloth, but mostly the dollars of the Silver Queen. To my surprise, although they knelt before the emperor, they put their gifts before General Ali or Empress Menen. I saw from their actions where the true power lay in Gondar. My great-uncle was an emperor as caged as his lions.

I kept my gaze on the ground when the chiefs walked by me, but I do not think I imagined it that many of them studied me carefully as they passed—as carefully as any village father looking for a bride for his son. I wanted to shrink away from their gazes that were like lizards' tongues.

When the priests came with their gorgeous, brilliant umbrellas, I looked for the face of my teacher. But all I could see were swirling colors, so many that I became dizzy. I stared beyond them at the yellow maskal flowers fastened to the tall wooden poles. What could be the explanation for my brother's absence?

Finally, as the last priests passed us, I admitted it to myself—Mesfin had to be in trouble. I remembered the sound of Empress Menen's voice and I shivered.

While torches turned the bonfire to a blazing sun that night, while people danced in ecstasy before the fire, while other girls and women filled the air with the *li-li-li* of joy cries, I stood as if I were a stool made out of wood. My joy had fallen to pieces as surely as had my emama's pot. In its place was a choking fear.

And the very next morning, my fear would turn to terror.

14 *Wax and Gold*

The day started calmly enough. We put ashes on our foreheads in the shape of the cross and said to one another, "Praise God who has brought you safely into the new year."

I knew my teacher was a careful man and would say nothing rash, so when he came to instruct me, I made my question equally careful. "My interest in history has grown," I told him. "When did the emperors of Gondar lose their great authority?"

"With Emperor Tekle Giorgis II," he said.

Ah. My grandmother's father.

"He created a very unpopular tax on honey," my teacher went on, careful in return. "The nobles of the land did not want to pay it. They went to the general who sat at the emperor's right hand and said they would support him as long as they did not have to pay the tax. Since then, it is the generals who have had the greatest authority in Gondar."

"Enough authority to put emperors on the throne and pull emperors off the throne?"

He did not say yes, but he did not say no.

For a moment, I wondered why the generals did not simply put themselves on the throne. But then I remembered that great destruction would come if Ethiopia ever had a ruler who was not descended from King Solomon and the Queen of Saba. Yet I had seen for myself that my great-uncle, the emperor, was like the azmari's doll that danced for a fiddle bow.

"Here's a riddle," my teacher said carefully. "Who has more power? A hyena or the mother who gave birth to the hyena?"

I stared at the floor, trying to think about what he was telling me.

After a moment, my teacher went on. "Ali was only twelve years old when the generals and chiefs in Debre Tabor decided he would become the head over all of them." His voice was so soft, I had to lean close to hear. "So young that in reality his mother ruled for the next ten years. What tastes does a mother develop when her twelve-year-old son is the most powerful person in the land?"

"The taste to become empress?" My heart frightened me with its drumbeat.

"Where would she stop? Would she seek to marry a man the people kept saying was destined to become emperor? If this man already had a wife, would such a hyena stop at poison? Might such a man have to flee with his two young children?"

I gaped at him, horrified. A stuttering drum pounded in my head. I . . . no. Wait. He couldn't be saying that . . . My ears would refuse to hear such a thing. My heart would refuse to understand. No. No. No.

"Forgive me," he said abruptly. "I have said too much." He stood and rushed from the room.

I stared after him, pain and fury twisting me like a cloth. I must not think about what he had said. I needed help. What did the hyenas have planned for my brother and me now that they had found us again? Where *was* my brother?

The silence was jolted by a great clattering and yelling outside my window. When I rushed to look, the first person I saw was General Ali, mounted on his horse and shouting at his guards. The courtyard between the castles was filled with soldiers on their horses and mules. To one side, I saw the azmaris, playing their instruments and putting poetry to music. They always sang the truth of what they saw.

"What the heart will not see, the eye cannot see," Emama had often said. With new eyes, I studied General Ali. My teacher once said the general had been powerful for such a long time that he rarely became angry or upset about anything.

But today he was both angry and upset.

I felt someone's presence at my elbow. It was the girl who carried my umbrella, whose aunt was one of the azmaris. "Please, lady. We should not be at the window now," she said, but her own gaze was fixed on what was happening below.

I did not move. We stood and watched what seemed to be some kind of disagreement between General Ali and his most trusted soldiers, the palace guards. After a while, the azmaris began to sing, making people laugh. The women of Gondar were famous for their poetry and songs, and the girl's aunt began to sing out line after line, while the azmari men responded to each line with a chorus of their own.

By now I knew why I sometimes had a hard time understanding what the azmaris sang. It was the art of wax and gold. The goldsmiths made models out of wax and covered the wax in clay. Then they heated the clay to make the wax melt and run out. Finally, they poured in molten gold.

Thus it was, my teacher had said, with certain poems and songs. Words or phrases could mean more than one thing, and azmaris were masters at playing with these double meanings. The obvious meaning was like the wax mold. But a person skilled in such poetry—listening carefully—could also hear the hidden gold.

This morning, I tried to make my ears separate the wax from the gold. "When lions and elephants fight," the musicians sang, "it is the mice who must tremble."

"Tell me what's happening," I ordered the girl.

She spoke hesitantly, and both my eyes and my heart began to see. She told me that all the kings and nobles of Ethiopia were fighting against each other, but no one of them was strong enough to unite the whole country under his power. The land was in such tumult that many peasants had simply abandoned their villages and were wandering the roads and countryside, begging from or attacking rich travelers.

"When the mice dig ditches," the musicians sang, "the birds of prey starve."

"The soldiers," she said, "survive by going to the peasants and seizing corn and grain. The farmers fight back by hiding the grain. These are the things they are singing about."

After a while, made bold by the laughter of the people, the azmaris began to sing about General Ali. They sang that he had not crushed his enemies when he had had the chance, and many of the nobles of Gondar had not paid proper tribute on Maskal. Even his own relatives were threatening to rise up and support a new ruler.

I watched and listened with fascination to the

directness of these stings. All of the people standing
around were enjoying the azmaris' antics. As for
General Ali, although it might be true that he was
seldom angry, I could see that the actions of some of
his guards and the songs of the azmaris were making
him furious.

When the servants brought food to my room,
I moved away from the window and tried to eat,
shivering with bitterness and anguish. *Ayezosh,*
I whispered to myself. *You must let your heart see.*

I forced myself to remember my teacher's exact
words. "If this man already had a wife, would such
a hyena stop at poison?" He had to be talking about
Empress Menen, the mother of the man outside my
window now. He had to mean that the empress was
determined enough to poison my own mother in
hopes of marrying my royal father. Now it was my
turn, poor spider, to squirm under the hyena's foot.

And my brother? I realized bitterly that I had been
so wrong in thinking he was being trained to be the
next emperor. The hyenas had no reason to want a
popular ruler anywhere near Gondar's throne. Empress

Menen wanted the throne for herself, and General Ali wanted a tame emperor on the throne.

I finally saw the truth of why we had been brought to Gondar. Anyone who found my father or brother would have a powerful weapon on his side. These hyenas did not want my brother to fall into the enemies' hands. And trading me in marriage could gain them more power. So, where *was* my brother? Would they . . . no. I could not think such a terrible thing.

Suddenly, a loud shouting made me drop my food and step back to the window.

"The table needs a strong man at its head," the azmaris were singing now. "But when the servants call the master to dinner, they discover he has gone on a long journey."

Before I had time to ask what that meant, I saw that some of the guards had dismounted from their horses. They were lying on the ground, refusing to move. Beside me, I heard the girl gasp. I stared, my whole body tight as an azmari's fiddle bow.

"No one can find the master to tell him the feast

is in his honor," a musician sang. I was completely puzzled. For a moment, even the azmaris were silent. The whole place seemed to hang twirling on an angel's string, waiting for the thunder.

It came so quickly that nobody had time to duck or hide. I saw General Ali's arm drop in a terrible motion. I saw his mouth move. And in one awful moment, I saw the soldiers on horseback obey his command.

The courtyard was a mass of trampling horses and screaming people.

"No," the girl cried out beside me. "Stop them!"

"Stop!" I screamed. But my voice was drowned by the sound of her wailing.

The girl fell, like a stone dropped from the hand of a horseback rider. I knelt beside her, calling for help.

Even as I shouted, I knew there were people outside who would need help even more than this girl did.

15 Horror

As I knelt beside her, the girl uttered frightful cries. "She sounds just like a hyena," I heard a servant whisper. "Clearly under the influence of a buda."

I was not so sure. The sounds coming out of her mouth were ones my own mouth was longing to make. "Is her aunt still alive?" I asked urgently. "Send someone down to find out." Had General Ali punished not only his guards but—like that other general a hundred years before—also the truth-speaking azmaris?

Now the girl lay completely still. One of the other servants pinched her, but she did not even twitch. Her thumbs were curled tightly in her fists. "Her thumbs belong to the buda," a servant whispered.

I tried to pry her thumbs out, but she had astonishing strength. A rustling at the door made me look up.

Praise be to God! It was the girl's aunt, looking stunned but alive. "All the musicians ran," she stammered to me. "Some of the guards are dead. I do not know how many."

As soon as she had taken the girl away, I slipped out and fled from the castle, through the Gate of the Pigeons, and away from the terror and confusion of the compound. I hardly knew what I needed, but I needed something. Some comfort. Some wisdom. I did not stop until I had come to the church of Debre Birhan Selassie. I bowed and kissed its doorway quickly.

Once again, gazing up at the angel eyes stopped my trembling so that I could at least draw breath and think. Although I had not noticed it before, so swept up with the angels, I now saw that a powerful painting of Saint Giorgis the protector, dressed in red and gold and riding on his white horse, was near the ceiling, on the west wall. More than ever before in my life, I needed protection.

Saint Giorgis, I cried silently to him. He, slayer of dragons, must have seen just how ruthless the powerful could be. *I plead with you to come and help me. Surely, your horse could stop even the horses commanded by General Ali.*

Had I really understood my teacher's words about Empress Menen? Had I truly seen General Ali's mouth shape such deadly words? My anxiety about Mesfin turned to a river of fear that poured through my body, bouncing me from one thought to another the way pebbles bounced under a horse's hooves. Where was my brother? Was he helpless? Was he trapped by hyenas that could decide in an instant whether he would live or die? Perhaps they had carried him far away to some high amba.

What could I possibly do to help my brother? General Ali was not known for being a cruel or even an angry man, but he had thought nothing of using his power against his own guards when they refused to obey him. If a guard with a shield made of hippopotamus hide could not stand against the hyenas, how could I?

I heard the murmuring of the voices of priests at their devotions. The thick smell of incense comforted me in its blanket. I felt a touch on my shoulder and turned to see that it was my teacher. He did not say a word, but I saw compassion in his eyes. We walked back to the compound together, and I drew strength from his presence. For once, I had no questions to ask him. Just his familiar steps beside me were enough.

The land around us was beautiful. The pastures were still covered with their bright, beautiful carpets of yellow maskal flowers. Birds wheeled and called to each other in the vast blue sky. I heard the solemn clanking of a cowbell and the bleating of goats being driven to pasture by some boy that, just for a moment, I could imagine might be my own brother. The peace of the moment made the terror of the last hours seem unreal.

When we reached the castle, I said, "I think I have come to understand the lesson in the story you told me about the three boys in the forest." I paused, glancing around with a shudder to where the bodies still lay on the ground. "I will never again trust a powerful person."

He gave me a slight bow and turned to look at the same sad sight. The whole compound lay in eerie quiet except for the lions, which were pacing and growling in their house, no doubt stirred up by the smell of blood.

16 *The Kosso Seller's Son*

The castle was swirling with sound and motion when I walked inside. All of the servants were clearly upset and afraid. But General Ali had not reigned since he was twelve years old without gaining much cleverness. Having commanded bloody and swift punishment with one hand, he was now moving as swiftly to hold out a gift with the other hand to try to maintain—or regain—the loyalty of the rest of the soldiers.

He had declared that tomorrow there would be a feast for all of the soldiers. I wished they would refuse him, but I had seen how impossible it was to defy such power. I could hear the chop, chop, chopping sound of knives and smell hundreds of onions being minced for the wat.

That night was an anguished one. General Ali had

ordered the bodies of the dead left where they were, and the hyenas were drawn to the compound by the smell of death. No people dared to stir outside. This night there was no music. There was no poetry. There was only the weird whooping of the hyenas right outside my window.

I tossed in my bed, thinking once again about spiders who sat still on the walls, hoping not to be noticed, as lizard tongues flickered closer and closer. Perhaps it was the spirit of the empress who had built this castle so many years ago that came to me in the darkness. She must have once been as horrified as I was, watching a general give an order to kill azmaris. Finally, I sat straight up in the middle of the night, knowing I must not simply crouch under my gahbi, waiting for destruction, as I had done for a moment the night of the fire.

Before I could lose my courage, I searched under the bed and quickly found the things I had put there seemingly so long ago. Quietly, careful not to wake any of the servants, I pulled on my old clothes, lifted the torn shamma over my head, and took the leather bag in my hands.

Downstairs, I hesitated, overcome with my own boldness. Most nights, the compound was filled with sleeping soldiers, and there were watchmen at every gate. Tonight the compound belonged to the hyenas. The moment I stepped from the castle, I saw one nearby. It raised its head and growled. I was close enough to see its sharp teeth and the bristles on its neck.

I wanted to shriek out my terror and run back inside. But for the sake of my brother, I could not. Saint Giorgis himself must have been with me, because my hand did not shake as I took a piece of the dried meat from the leather bag and, just as I had thrown stones at the monkeys in our fields, I threw the meat close enough so the hyena could smell it. While the hyena's teeth tore at the meat, I was already through the gate.

Perhaps there was some person, somewhere in the city of Gondar, who could help me, but the severe emperor of old had gone to the countryside, and so did I. I fixed my gaze on a faraway shepherd's fire and walked by the moon's light, stumbling and tripping but always finding my way again.

When I neared the fire, I hung back for a while, watching the cloaked figures that huddled close to its warmth. The night I had tried to run away from the soldiers, I had seen how easy it was to appear and disappear in the darkness, and now I moved with care until I, too, was standing wrapped in my shamma with all of the other figures.

People glanced at me, but no one said anything. By my poor clothing, they no doubt assumed I was just another peasant. When I pulled some stale bread from my bag and shared it with those closest to me, people nodded their thanks. They gnawed at the bread, hard as it was. In these times, food was food.

The talk was of politics. What else? I heard the story of what I had seen that day from my window. I did not speak up to correct any of the information they shared, though the five or ten people who had died had grown to thirty and the horses had become a galloping regiment.

The things I learned around that fire! I heard, for the first time, the name of Kassa. "Kassa?" said a loud-

mouthed man, laughing. "What's that but a cure for
the worms that trouble our stomachs."

"Why laugh?" said the man who had spoken the
name. "What if his mother did sell kosso in the streets
when he was a child? He was a poor man, like us."

They talked on. I heard that this man, Kassa, had
gathered hundreds of men and many guns. He had
started as a robber, but one who lived simply among
his men. He ordered his men to stop taking food and
other goods from the peasants. "Why should we harm
the poor," he asked, "instead of the rich merchants
who travel through these lands?"

Kassa next turned his attention to lands his uncles
and brother had once tasted, or received tribute from.
General Ali had seized these lands and had given them
to his mother, Menen. I noticed that these men did not
call her "empress." When Kassa took back the lands his
relatives had tasted, Menen tried to subdue him. But
he was too brave, too bold. When she saw the power
he was gaining and how the people loved him, she
called him to Gondar and granted him the right
to rule over those lands. Even more surprising, she

arranged for Kassa to marry General Ali's beautiful and delicate daughter.

"And here is a surprise," Loudmouth said. "General Ali's daughter is devoted to her husband."

I leaned forward, listening. The speaker said that when Kassa received a serious wound in battle, Menen followed custom by sending some meat to speed his recovery. A man of Kassa's rank could have expected a whole bull. Instead, she sent only one leg of beef. "I heard," the man said, "that General Ali's daughter told her husband to stand up and not swallow this insult." This comment drew murmurs and chuckles of amazement.

So Kassa was the pinching hand, making General Ali and Empress Menen clutch frantically at their power. Kassa's boldness must be the reason they had become determined to root my brother and me from our place of safety.

"I say, let him come," the first man said. "Let him overthrow the emperors who have become like wilting flowers—Our Ladies, the Castle Keepers."

Everyone laughed.

Two more figures joined the group around the fire, one staggering under a load of wood. "Here," the man with the loud mouth said. "We could use that wood for the fire."

"May your eyes fall out if they even try to look upon my wood." It was a girl's voice, and a fierce one.

The men laughed again. "My brother's daughter will bite your fingers off," said her companion. "She's been gathering this wood to take to Gondar to sell. Hunger turns a person to stone, and one stone is enough against fifty clay pots."

I heard the clicks of assent. One stone *was* enough against fifty clay pots. No one moved toward the girl or her wood.

After a while, the uncle spoke again. "She's clumsy, but she works hard."

"I'm clumsy but I *do* work hard. I like to work," she agreed cheerfully.

"She likes to eat, too. No sooner do we manage to buy an egg than she eats it."

"Better to have an egg this year than a chicken next year."

I liked this girl. As silently as a shadow, I made my way around the fire until I was close to her. "I know where there is work and no hunger." I said the words very quietly so that only she could hear them. If she cried out or turned to the man to repeat what I had said, she was not the person for me.

"I like to work," she said again, her voice so soft that I almost thought I had imagined it.

Now Loudmouth launched into another story of what he called the strangest battle in Ethiopia. An enemy of General Ali managed to convince many Amharas that the general and his mother might pretend to be Christians but they still had Muslim hearts. Soon there was a battle.

"From where General Ali watched," the man said, "he saw many of his horsemen fall to the enemy guns. Believing the battle lost, he fled. But his enemy saw many of *his* men fall and also fled."

The men howled with laughter. It was obvious they knew this story, but I could tell that it amused them every time they heard it. The enemy general was the first to get the word that both leaders had fled, and he

returned and entered General Ali's house for a feast.
But one of the general's officers captured him there.
"There was only one problem," Loudmouth said. "No
one knew where General Ali was. They had to use
spies to find him and tell him that the power was his."

Now I understood how the azmaris had goaded
General Ali to fury when they sang about the feast.
In the laughter, I moved away from the fire. The girl
followed, though I had not told her to.

"When you take the wood to Gondar," I told her
softly, "go to the castle of the ancient empress. Ask
for the old servant who is like a grandmother to all
the other servants."

She barely moved and I could not see her face, but
I knew from the gesture she made with her hand that
she understood.

"Speak only to that woman. Tell her you have heard
that there is need of one to carry an umbrella. Give her
your wood as a gift."

We returned to the fire. Now the men had begun
to argue about whether Kassa had the blood of King
Solomon and the Queen of Saba. The loudmouthed

man was saying it had recently been discovered that he did. In the noise, I melted back into the night and set out for what had become my home.

17 *Spiders Unite*

By the next day, I had turned from a spider into a lion—pacing, growling, and snapping. I waited and waited for my teacher, but he did not come. Finally, full of impatience, I sent a servant to find the old woman who told me, "He had to leave Gondar quickly because his mother is ill." I did not believe this, but it didn't matter. Now my only hope was the girl.

"Find someone who can carry my umbrella. I want to go outside," I told her, making my voice as much like the voice of Empress Menen as I could.

"The women are very busy today," she said. "As you know, General Ali has ordered a huge feast for all the soldiers."

Good. It was just as I wanted it. I did my best to show her my displeasure.

Finally, I saw the girl coming with her load of wood. From the window, I tried to see if I was making a foolish mistake to trust such a person with my life. She was thinner than I remembered last night, but I saw the determination in her stance that I had heard in her voice last night. I watched as she stumbled on a stone, dropping her wood. Then she argued for a moment with one of the servants. When I saw that the old woman was going out to speak to the girl, I hurried to my bed and pretended to be resting.

They would need the wood for all the cooking that was being done. I could smell the onions and butter and the hot spices that made me sneeze. Then I heard footsteps and the polite cough of the old woman.

At first, I kept my face turned away. I did not rise until the girl had tripped on the rug and knelt by my bed. "She could carry your umbrella," the old woman said. Now that I had turned into a lion, she was anxious to please me.

"What is your name?" I asked the girl.

"Negatwa." Her voice was muffled because her head was down.

Her name meant "the coming of the dawn." *May God make you the coming of dawn to me*, I said to myself. "Stand up," I said aloud to her.

She did not look directly into my eyes, of course. A person would never do that to her elders or someone in authority. I saw her gaze flick across my face, though. She would not have seen me well in the darkness by the fire, but surely she recognized my voice. I waited for her face to betray me. She gave no sign.

"She is clumsy," I said, "but I suppose she may carry my umbrella. Get her some clean clothes."

I did not dare talk in the castle. "Come," I told Negatwa when she reappeared. "I wish to go to church."

I forced myself to walk slowly, as I had learned important people must. Inside I was trembling, but I must not show that if I had any dream of surviving. Finally, I had the hope of sharing my questions with one other person. As Emama often said, "For one person, fifty lemons are a burden. For fifty persons, fifty lemons are sweet smells."

We had almost reached the gate when I heard a voice that made the blood inside of me turn thick. It was the empress.

Remembering the girl who had taken bread from me so long ago, I went to Empress Menen immediately and knelt to touch my head to her feet. Although I was not sure of how to greet the empress, I knew that lower was certainly better. But what was she doing out of her castle?

"Where are you going?" Her voice was cold and suspicious.

"I go to kiss Saint Giorgis," I told her meekly.

There was a dreadful silence. "See that you come right back," she finally said. "Here." She called one of the nearby soldiers over. "Go with her to Debre Birhan Selassie."

When we reached the church, I told the soldier to stay at the gate. Fortunately, he obeyed. As soon as Negatwa and I were among the junipers, I began to pour out my story in a low voice. It might not be wise to give Negatwa all of this information, but what else could I do? I needed to find my brother, and there was nobody else to turn to. And even if the help was from someone who was even more helpless than I was, hadn't both Emama and my brother said that spiders could tie up a lion?

I was relieved to see that she seemed to quickly understand. "Servants always talk among themselves," she told me. "Let me see if anyone knows anything about your brother."

As we entered Debre Birhan Selassie, kissing the doorway, she whispered, "The forty-four churches of Gondar are famous for giving sanctuary. We can start by seeing whether he has been able to flee to one of them."

That thought gave me hope. A priest approached us and I knelt to kiss his cross. Overhead, the angels soared and sang their song of comfort. To one side, Saint Giorgis's horse towered over me, as if I could seek shelter between its hooves. But then I saw something that made all my new confidence fly.

Saytan! The most evil of all evil beings.

The artist had painted him on one of the walls.

He was glossy black, with huge glaring eyes and horns. A third ear stood right up in the middle of his forehead. His massive feet each had six claws. He sat in the midst of flames, hugging the fire with his two arms. But what really made me shudder was that he had a girl's head caught between his teeth.

The priest, seeing where I was looking, said, "When Saytan was roaming the earth as he is allowed to do every thousand years, the girl fell in love with him."

"With Saytan?"

"Yes. It may seem impossible, but she was young and easily fooled. Before she had time to get older and gain wisdom, she died and went to heaven. Even then, she longed to be with Saytan, so she knelt before God and asked whether it was possible for Saytan to come to heaven."

I closed my eyes. It was obvious that, instead, God had sent her to be where Saytan was. And now she was condemned to stay between his ferocious teeth for all of eternity.

My heart was so full of the evil thing I saw on that wall that even the angels could not give me strength that day. Perhaps it was a warning from the saints themselves, because immediately after, disaster fell upon my head.

As we left the church, Negatwa said to the soldier, "Now my lady will go to kiss Saint Mikael." And we were well on the path toward another of the churches when we heard someone calling.

The soldier held up his hand. "It is not a robber," he said, "but another soldier."

For one panicked moment, I wanted to run. But I knew how quickly a girl could be overcome by a soldier.

The news he carried was just as I feared. "Empress Menen orders that the girl come back to the castle at once."

I was filled with foreboding. Saytan had deceived a young girl into falling in love with him, but she still received a terrible punishment. After the strangest battle in Ethiopian history was over, nothing had changed—except for the soldiers and peasants who had died in the battle. Lions and elephants fought, and it was the mice and spiders that were caught.

When we reached the castle, the old woman was there to meet me. I could tell with one glance at her face that I did not want to hear what she was going to tell me. "The Empress Menen tells us that arrangements are being made for your marriage, my lady." She looked away, using a formal tone I had never before heard from her.

Mice and spiders. The empress had given her own granddaughter in marriage to a man she despised. Now she was sending soldiers against that man. I was not sure about what the hyena's plans were for me, but I was sure those plans would not have anything to do with my happiness. No doubt in these turbulent times, she was trying to tie some other powerful man to her through me.

"Unless this wedding is planned for this very day," I said, "why may I not take myself to church?"

The old woman sighed. "Negotiations are at a delicate stage. You must stay inside the castle until the empress sends for you herself."

"And when will that be?" I asked angrily. "On my wedding day?"

From the way the old woman guided me stiffly up the stairs, I guessed that was just about right. Now my home had become my prison.

18 *Caught Between Saytan's Teeth*

All day I lay on my bed, refusing to eat. Negatwa and the old woman brought buttery wat and sugar cakes and almonds and figs to tempt me, but I only turned away from them. I would be like the soulless horse.

"How can you give up?" Negatwa finally whispered to me. "You at least are imprisoned in a castle. What if your brother is on top of a high amba with only the wind and clouds to hear his cries? What hope does he have, except for you?"

My brother was depending on me. It was a strange and new thought.

From then on, Negatwa was my eyes and ears. She went out when she could, but we also spent many long hours with our cotton, she at my feet. When I bent close to her so that she could show me something in the spinning, she would quietly tell me what she had discovered.

Unfortunately, for many days my eyes were blind and my ears were deaf. Negatwa started by going to all of the churches in the area. One of them, Debre Sahai, Mount of the Sun, had a roof that was covered with red cloth and mirrors so that it flashed magnificent praise to the sky. Negatwa's voice was filled with awe when she described the church to me. Even in Debre Sahai, though, the priests knew nothing of my brother.

Servants, soldiers, townspeople, and peasants talked to her willingly about what they did know. We discovered that Kassa was growing stronger daily. "I have heard different stories about who his father was," she said in her low voice. "Though his relatives definitely tasted the lands around Lake Dembya, his mother lived in Gondar in great poverty, selling kosso on the streets of the city. She sent her son to study at a monastery on the lake."

I thought of the water I had seen that day so long ago when I rode to Gondar. Many churches and monasteries sat on Lake Dembya's islands, my teacher had told me. Had a frightened young Kassa once traveled the same path that brought my brother and me to this city?

"Do you remember that night by the fire, when the man talked about the strangest battle in Ethiopian history?" Negatwa asked. "During that battle, soldiers burned the monastery where Kassa was studying, but he escaped. That's when he became a bandit, robbing the rich traders."

So it was the injustice he had seen that drove him to be a bandit. I hoped that even now his soldiers were defeating the soldiers of the empress. "What do the people say about him?" I asked.

"They say he learned to love books and Ethiopian

history from his stay in the monastery. And from being a bandit, he learned to lead men. But they say the empress despises him, always calling him 'the kosso seller's son.'"

The people said General Ali and his mother were doing everything they could to stop Kassa, but more men flocked to his side every day. And even though he was related to the general and the empress by marriage, Kassa was pressing on. I sniffed scornfully. The so-called empress had brought much of her trouble on herself.

One afternoon, Negatwa came rushing into my room. She moved carefully around the carpet that always grabbed her feet, but I could see she was bursting with news. Her arms and shoulders wiggled as she took out my ivory spindle from the basket, gave it to me, and settled at my feet. As I leaned down to hear what she had to say, she gave me a triumphant smile.

"My brother?" I could hardly breathe.

"No." For a moment she was downcast. Then she brightened. "But I have found another person from your family, long lost."

"Emama?" I wanted to leap and sing. I knew she would find her way to Gondar if I only gave her long enough. She would not be able to see me now, of course, but Negatwa would carry word to her, and maybe she would have an idea about my impending marriage or about my brother.

"No." Now Negatwa hung her head.

"Who?" I demanded.

"Your father."

My father. Even though I had heard the empress talk about him, I did not really think of him as being alive. And he probably did not know I was alive.

"What did you hear about him?" I whispered.

"The news is everywhere among the people that he has found his way to Kassa's camp," Negatwa said. "More and more people are saying 'Let Kassa come.' They are ready for change."

So a bird had escaped from a snake. God willing, maybe a spider could as well.

Then came a time of silence. Every day when Negatwa came back from her errands, I could see by the way she held her shoulders that she had heard nothing new. To distract ourselves, we talked of other things. She told me about the day when soldiers swept through the place where her family had their house and land.

The soldiers had come often for many years, demanding goats and bread and lodging. After one particularly good growing season, the farmers had come up with a plan. They dug a pit in the middle of a field and plastered the bottom and sides of it with mud until it was smooth inside. The next time word came from relatives in a far-off village that soldiers were on the way, people rushed to put their grain and other things inside the pit.

The pit was covered with wood and then earth was laid on top of it. "My father and the others then ploughed over the top of the pit," Negatwa said. "He told me that even he, who had seen it, could not tell where the mouth of the pit was. But the soldiers became angry to find so little grain from any of the farmers. The farmers and soldiers fought each other. My father . . . he—" She stopped, then started again, ". . . and my mother . . ."

She leaned her head against the side of the bed and did not go on speaking. I could guess the ending of this story, and we sat, grieving together, for some time.

With both of her parents gone and the lands around her home in uproar, her uncle brought Negatwa to Gondar with him. Because the forests near Gondar had all been cut down for firewood for Gondar's houses and palaces, there was a great need for people who would go far away and bring wood to sell. That was how she had been managing to eat.

"Here at least you have plenty of food," I said. "And you do not have to bend your back under the weight of the wood."

"Here I am filled with joy," she agreed quickly. "You have become my new mother."

I laughed at that, seeing as we were surely about the

same number of years on the earth. But although it felt good to laugh together, I wondered what would happen to her when the time for my dreaded marriage came.

>≈

Then came a week when the air seemed to be drenched with fear. A weasel had scratched its way into the House of the Pigeons and killed most of the birds, so the days were oddly silent. Negatwa brought back news—or new rumors—every day. We were never sure what the truth was. One day she heard that the soldiers of General Ali and Empress Menen had completely vanquished Kassa and he was being dragged back to Gondar in chains. The next day she heard that this was not so at all. Instead, Kassa had captured the leader of the soldiers and made him drink kosso until he died—in revenge for the empress's taunts.

In Gondar, the bodies of the men that had been trampled were long gone, but hyenas still lurked around the edges of the compound at night. Now that they were hungrier, they were fiercer than ever, and the night's silence was broken by the hyenas' howls. Some nights I thought I would soon join them in their cries. Hearing nothing about my brother made me melancholy, and even a little fierce.

Eventually the day came that I had feared. I had told Negatwa to take our spun cotton to one of the weavers to have a new shamma made for her, so she had gone off joyously. She came back quietly. "The news is about you, my lady," she said.

I let my fingers play in the cotton, trying to calm myself. "Tell me."

"The general and the empress are strengthening ties with a prince of another region. A merchant told me that this prince would soon march north with his soldiers and end the threat of Kassa for the last time," Negatwa said.

At the same time, General Ali was reaching out to a lifetime enemy, a man who ruled most of northern Ethiopia and was none other than the other general who had run from the strangest battle in Ethiopian history. If all else failed, the two of them would join their armies into an unbeatable force that would surely crush Kassa.

"And what is my part in all of this?" I asked.

"Some say you are to be married to a son of this prince," she said. "Others say no, no, it is to the son of that general. But all say that it will take place on the first day of next week."

Next Wednesday. Now my doom had indeed come down upon my head. I was to be like the girl with her head caught in Saytan's teeth.

19 Song of the Dawn Singers

That night, I didn't sleep.

O Gondar, I thought. Both majestic and stealthy, full of whispering servants. Both beautiful and terrible. Luxurious and falling to pieces. What was going to happen to Gondar? What was going to happen to me? I remembered again the soulless horse. There was more than one way to respond to prison. The horse had refused to eat or drink, the servant said. Could I not do the same?

In the hour before the sun hatched from its dark shell, I listened to the songs of the *lalibelotch*, the dawn singers. Most of them were lepers and thus could not mix with other people, for fear that others would catch the skin disease that chewed their faces and hands. Just before dawn each morning, they would stand like shadows, wrapped in shammas so that only their eyes could be seen, and sing at the gates of the rich.

This morning, the songs seemed particularly sad and mournful. As I listened, I felt tears gather in the corners of my eyes. I knew what I must do. Before I lost my courage, I would go to Negatwa's room and tell her to find some poison. I would die as my mother had surely died.

The singing died away. One of the servants had no doubt been sent to the gate with scraps of food for the lalibelotch. In a few moments, dawn would leap into the sky. The lalibelotch would slip away.

I sighed and roused myself from the bed. Feeling like an old woman, I moved stiffly out of my room and into the next. But Negatwa was not lying on her bed. So.

She must have decided it was better to go back to being a wood carrier than to be dragged far away to a strange place with me and never see the mountains of her home again. I did not hold this against her, but now I would have to come up with a new plan for getting the poison.

I shuffled out of her room and went to lie down on my bed again to think of who now would be willing to help me. My stomach was so full of such feelings of gloom that I paid no attention to the person who came into my room a few moments later.

"My lady."

I sat right up with joy. "It is you. You did not go away from me!"

"Only to speak to one of the lalibelotch." She rushed forward and fell to her knees by the bed. "Yesterday, I stumbled in the street and dropped the package I was carrying. A man stooped to help me and whispered that I should go to the lalibelotch this morning. I would have told you before, but he said I should say nothing to any person if I valued your life."

I stared at her. This was dire indeed. How had she

had the courage to approach those shadow figures, when no one dared get close to a leper? Even the sons and daughters of lepers—who often did not have the same disease, the servants said—usually kept to themselves and never went near strangers. I was ashamed that I had doubted Negatwa's loyalty.

She glanced over her shoulder. No one else was awake or stirring yet, but still she spoke in the softest voice. "The man told me to bring you word from your teacher. The empress sent him far away. But he did not forget about you," Negatwa said. "When your teacher heard of your marriage, he managed to make his way back to Gondar. He bade me tell you that he is willing to meet you in the dark of night, after the moon goes down tomorrow. He will have mules, and if you like, he will help you make your way to sanctuary. When the lalibelotch sing before the roosters bring in tomorrow's dawn, I must go to him with your answer."

I had to force the next words from my mouth. "Did you ask him about my brother?"

She would not look at me. "He said to tell you that God will console you. That you are under the protection

of God and the earth. That your brother is in the belly
of the hyena. He said you would understand."

All that day, I cried.

"May God console you," Negatwa whispered, over
and over. God did not console me but, because I had
not slept the night before, tiredness finally overcame
me. I woke in the middle of the night, moaning. With
the wails of the hyenas in my ears, I mourned my
brother as I had the death of my grandfather. I had lost
Ababba, Emama, and now Mesfin, and even now that
I might escape my dreaded marriage, it was terrible to
think about going on completely alone.

In the early morning when the singing began, I sent
my answer. "Tell my teacher that I will accept his help,
but not to go to sanctuary," I said to Negatwa. "I want
to go to Empress Menen's enemy. To Kassa. There at
least I will find my father. Ask my teacher if he can
help me to get to Kassa's camp."

The answer came back in one word. "Yes."

20 *Riding the Soulless Horse*

We would have to get out of the compound at night again, and the hyenas were hungry. "It will be very dangerous," I told Negatwa. She agreed, shuddering. In her village, she told me, the girls would join together to go out to gather wood. One evening when they were coming back, a hyena caught a young girl at the end of the line and tore her nose from her face.

We clung to each other for a moment, horrified of what we were about to do. "I will go and get as much dried meat as I can," Negatwa said. "The cooking is done in many different houses around this compound. Perhaps I can get each cook to give me a little. I will say it is for your long journey, where you must go far from home, and they will have pity on you."

I forced myself to walk through the day as if it were

like any other day. Little by little the egg would walk—but not if she gave away her plan too soon. When it came time for the evening meal, I did not want to eat, but I knew I must. What Negatwa had told the cooks was true. Our journey would be a long one.

As she usually did, Negatwa served me, and I fed her bites of wat and injera from my own basket. Before she would let me drink, she always cupped a little honey water in her palm and tasted it. "A person never knows where enemies lurk," she often told me. "And poison has been the end of many born with royal blood."

After we were too full to eat any more, she carried the scraps away, where the servants would eat them. She was gone for a long time. When she returned, her face was stricken.

"Tell me." Now that the time for our escape was almost upon us, a strange calm had wrapped itself around my shoulders. I knew it was time to say my prayers and put myself into the hands of God.

"When I stepped outside just now," she said, "a man seized my arm. He had been waiting for me. He, too, has a plan. But this is a different one.

And it has to do with your brother."

My brother. I felt a giant hand squeeze all the breath out of me. He was still alive? There was news? I seized her fingers. "Tell me. Do not let a single word escape."

As darkness settled in the room, we did not light a candle. The man had not identified himself, but Negatwa thought he was one of the palace guards. He told her that his cousin had been killed the day General Ali's horses had trampled some of the men.

"So he wants revenge," I said.

"He plans to flee to Kassa's camp tonight. He did not tell me how he managed it, but after many weeks of searching, he found out where your brother is. And—" She uncurled her fingers. In the palm of her hand I could make out the dark shape of a key.

I snatched it from her. A fluttering cloth danced in my chest. One end of it was woven from excitement. The other was woven from dread.

"Wait," she said. "Consider this. The lock that fits this key is in a solitary and dangerous place."

"Even if it was in the stomach of the earth, I would go there for my brother," I told her.

"It is close to the stomach."

My brother was imprisoned where one of the rivers fell into a gorge, she told me, and the falling water hid a cave. "The empress has long used that cave to store some of the Silver Queen dollars that people give her for tribute. Now, the man said, she is using it to hold other treasure."

"And you think that treasure is my brother?"

"I'm sure of it."

For a long time, we sat in thought. We talked, and then our voices died away, and then we sat up to talk some more.

The man had explained where the gorge was, Negatwa said. It was not too far. Finally, we decided that first Negatwa must help me find the right place. Then she would leave me to go to our appointed spot to meet my teacher. She would ask him to wait just one hour. I would go alone into the fearful place close to the earth's stomach.

But first, we had to get past the hyenas.

The moon rose early and bright. We had to wait for it to sink back in the western sky before we dared to creep down the stairs. While we waited, Negatwa fixed a tiny leather bag around my neck. "The key is in there," she whispered. "And a knife, in case your brother is bound with some kind of cord."

I did not dare think ahead to that moment. Tonight we would risk such a simple thing. Breath. Life. I concentrated on her fingers brushing against my neck. Even if I died this night, I was glad to have met a girl with such loyalty and courage.

We settled back. We said our prayers. "Come," Negatwa finally said. "Look how dark the window has become. I think it's time."

Carefully we left the room, our bare feet not making a sound on the stones. Carrying my berebaso and the old leather bag the soldiers had given me, I moved ahead of her and started down the stairs. She had already put herself in much danger for me. Now I should be the one to face danger first.

The large castle seemed to breathe in its sleep. In its many rooms, the servants would have their eyes closed by now and would hear nothing until morning, when a great shout would go up. "She's gone! The spider has scampered away."

I knew these steps so well by now that my feet found their own way to the door. I paused. Outside, I heard a lion's grumble. Somewhere from just beyond the Gate of the Pigeons, a hyena's voice rose in a plaintive wail. Then, behind me, I heard a softer sound. Negatwa gasped.

I turned. Coming through the door behind me was the old woman. She held a burning candle, and for a long moment she and I looked at each other.

I found my voice first. "For the sake of my father," I whispered.

What could she do? It was a risk of her own life if she let me go. We simply watched each other. I was sure she would send up a cry that would bring the soldiers running. But then she bowed slightly, and as the candlelight lit her face, I saw that she had tears on her cheek. "And for your grandmother," she whispered. "I served her when I was only a child. May God give your feet speed."

My feet would need speed. Negatwa knelt and put the berebaso securely on them. She stood, and we pulled the meat from our bags. Almost before I could breathe, we were out under the stars and the slipping moon. The night air was thick and cold. Softly and quickly we went to the gate, where my teacher had paid the guard some amount of gold so that he would look the other way. We rushed through. The hyenas' wails rose in a chorus. "Hurry," Negatwa panted. "Just throw it."

We threw the meat frantically, and ran.

In my worst fears, I had never imagined I would run headlong through the dark night, not caring what my feet hit, not even pausing when tree branches caught my arms and made them bleed. Negatwa and I ran until I could not take another step. "I think we have left the hyenas behind," she said.

I shivered. "Quickly, then. Show me where I need to go."

Negatwa had been outside in the dark many times
since she had fled from her home, and she took my
hand, leading me forward. Every time she stumbled, I
winced. As soon as I heard the rustle of running water,
I asked, "Is this the place?"

"No. We turn here."

As we groped our way, a breeze blew up, making my
shamma flap against my face. For some reason, it made
me think of that long-ago day at the stream. I had been
afraid of a zar. I should have been afraid of humans and
their plans instead. "Is this it?" I asked again.

"Just a little bit farther. We need to go down into
this gorge. Hold my shoulder."

I might as well have been blind and lame, but
Negatwa's feet, for once, were sure. In a little while,
we stood silently, listening to the churning water,
searching in the dim light for the cave.

Negatwa touched my arm. "There, my lady." I
squinted and took a step, but then I turned back to
Negatwa.

"Here." I took off my berebaso and put them in her
hands. "It will be better for my feet to be bare, and

these will protect yours a little as you hurry to tell my teacher to wait. You have been my good friend, Negatwa, and I—"

I felt her fingers close around the sandals. "Yes," she said, not allowing me to continue.

"May they speed and protect your feet from stumbling," I finally said. "If my teacher doesn't see us soon, he must assume we've been caught. It will be too dangerous for him to linger."

I listened for a moment to the sounds of Negatwa scrambling back the way we had come. With the light from the stars, I could faintly see what I needed to do. The ledge wasn't terribly narrow or long. In the rainy season, it would be treacherous with the water thundering over the edge, making the rocks slippery. Even now, I could feel the spray on my face and knew I would have to stay close to the wall of rock.

We'd had to wait so long for the moon to go down that it must be close to midnight by now. At noon and midnight, the world belonged to Saytan. And Saytan liked nothing better than a water and forest place like this. I clutched my cross and felt my fingers tremble against my neck.

For one shaking moment, I thought of turning around and climbing back up the hill by myself. Perhaps I could find my father and he could come back here with me to rescue my brother. Or the priest would come. He would know some holy words.

In my stomach, I knew this could never be. Something was quickly devouring the hours of the night. Now was when my brother needed to be saved.

I put a foot on the cold ledge. My right hand reached for the wet wall behind it. The feel of the soft moss and solid stone steadied me. I pulled my second foot up. Cautiously, I began my awful journey.

In a few long moments, I was actually behind the waterfall. My clothes became wet with the drops that were being flung at me by some giant, unseen hand. The roar in my ears was louder than that of a thousand horses galloping down a slope. "Soulless horses," I whispered to myself. "Ayezosh."

I took a step. Then another. And another.

Suddenly, a weird wailing rose from the rocks. I shrieked, my voice drowned by the thundering water. I was falling, falling into the rock-black darkness.

No.

Wait.

My bare feet still felt hardness under them. My right hand still touched the same clump of soft, damp moss. And the wailing was only wind, I told myself. Only wind.

Holy Mariam. Kind Saint Giorgis.

I could hear my breath coming in ragged gasps.

What had the azmari sung about my grandfather on that day I came to Gondar? He was not afraid of spears or swords or even cannons. Had I not inherited my blood and bones from such a man?

It was mostly not a good thing to be born related to an emperor. I thought again of the questions my teacher had answered for me. My father had fled rather than stay and rule as Menen's husband. So Menen brought Yohannes III down from Amba Wehni to put him upon the throne.

That day, a herald would have stood in the town center pounding on the great drum forty-four times to give everyone time to gather. On the last beat, he would have begun shouting out the news. The old emperor was gone. But farmers should continue to farm. Traders should continue to trade. Friends should be happy and enemies should fear, "for we are Yohannes III, King of Kings."

My father, hiding somewhere, must have heard that drum and known that Menen had finally gotten what she wanted. If I ever found him, I would ask my father about that night. But here I stood, rooted to the wet rocks with fear. The wailing sound whined in my ears again. I dropped to the ledge on my hands and knees and then lay flat and still, as if I would cling to the rocks forever. *Saytan, do not scrape me off.* I let out one last despairing cry.

Why despair? Under the sounds of tumbling water, I heard these words as surely as if someone spoke them aloud. Had not my mother and father given Mesfin and me up so that we could live? Had not Emama and Ababba cradled Mesfin and me? On the night when my great-uncle was crowned, had not my mother's parents decided to find an even safer place, far from any village?

And just tonight, had not the old servant blessed me and let me go? Had not a soldier or guard risked his own life to give me a key? Empress Menen had most surely killed my mother, and now she wanted the rest of my family in her belly. But there was other protection. Time and time again, love and loyalty had surrounded me and kept me from the jaws of death.

As I lay there, feeling my whole body quivering against the wet rocks, I remembered standing in the church of Debre Birhan Selassie, beneath the angels and facing Saint Giorgis. My brother had always called me a dreamer. Well, then, let me dream. In front of me, Saint Giorgis was galloping, galloping. The thunderous sound was only his horse's hooves, protecting me.

Saytan crouched on another of the walls. But above him, angels hovered. Over my head and all around my shoulders were thousands of angels. More than that. Countless angels. I thought I could feel their wings flicking against my cheeks, encouraging me onward. Slowly, carefully, I wiggled my fingers forward on the cold rocks. And in this way—creeping slowly ahead— I moved the last few meters until I saw the iron gate that blocked the mouth of the cave.

My shaking fingers trembled for the key. I pulled myself up, using the bars, until I was standing again. Even with the thundering sound behind me, I could hear the clink, clink as my shivering tapped the key against the iron. Then it was sliding into the lock. I was pulling the door open.

Inside, the cave smelled dank and old. "Mesfin," I said in a low voice. "Are you there?"

"Saba?" His voice did not sound far away. My fumbling at the gate must have awakened him. He would have been lying in the darkness, caught between fear and hope, perhaps making himself ready for death. "Can it be you?"

"Can you see the stars?" I asked. "Can you move toward me?"

"My hands and feet are tied."

"Then talk to me until I can find my way to you."

Using the sound of his voice, I groped forward until I almost fell over him. At least he was wrapped in a thick blanket. Perhaps one of the guards had brought it to him. "How great is my joy!" I said as my fingers found his face. "Now maybe my fingers can see well enough in the dark to find your feet."

"When spiders unite," he said weakly, "they can tie up a lion."

I smiled at his words as my fingers fumbled for the knife. "It is not tying we need now," I said, "but exactly the opposite."

A short time later, my teacher and I sat on our mules. My brother had insisted that he could ride his own mule, though he looked unsteady to me. "Let him try it," my teacher said. "He can ride behind me when his weakness overcomes his resolve."

Just now, Mesfin sat on the ground, gathering his strength, while Negatwa dug in the leather bags for food. She would start out on my mule, her arms around my waist. This time, I would be the one to sit in front.

"We should begin very soon," my teacher said to me. "But first think about this one last time, Saba. Are you sure you want to go forward into a strange land? I could take your brother to Kassa, but you could still turn back and live a life of royalty married to a great prince or noble." I couldn't see his face in the darkness, but his voice was serious. "You could have the title of princess."

I thought of everything I had learned about royalty. It was strange to me that General Ali and his mother were sometimes on the same side, joining hand to hand, power to power, while at other times, they circled warily like two wild animals ready to claw and bite each other to death. The people said that General Ali and his daughter loved each other deeply. Yet now the daughter was urging her husband, Kassa—someone she also loved—against her father and grandmother. And my great-uncle, Emperor Yohannes III, the only one among them who carried the blood of Solomon and Saba, was no more than a puppet.

I glanced down at the shadowy shapes on the ground. My brother. After we had made our careful way back across the ledge, we had stood, touching cheek to cheek, for a long moment before we began to walk. How great was my joy to have saved him from the cave. To be traveling with him again. No, the hyena life was not for me.

Perhaps mistaking my silence for uncertainty, my teacher pressed on. "If you go to Kassa, who knows what will become of you?"

It was true. I would have to be very careful, putting us under the protection of yet another hyena. But it was this hyena that would give me the best chance of finding my father and seeing my emama again. I pressed my legs against the saddle, feeling my own strength. "I am the great-granddaughter of an emperor," I said. "I have the blood and name of the Queen of Saba. And I am not afraid."

"You have great courage."

Did I? I looked up. The sky looked as if someone had taken a gourd full of stars and tipped it, spilling the stars like melted butter in a great smear across the darkness. No, I did not have great courage. But I had learned that fear was not fought in the stomach but simply by taking one stumbling step when it was needed.

"I know priests and others who will help us all along the way." My teacher reached down and patted the mule's neck. "There will be many places where we can hide and take food. But when we reach our destination, it will not be an easy thing—riding into a camp where nobody knows who we are. These are mistrustful times."

"Yes," I agreed. "I can see it will be a trip of danger with possibly an even more dangerous ending."

"If we do reach Kassa's gates," he said, "we must depend on you to explain why we have come. No doubt you will need to have someone quickly find your father, who can speak to Kassa on our behalf."

It was amazing. For so many months, I had longed for protection. Now I was a protector.

"Yes," I said again. "I can do it." Once, I thought being strong meant being like Saint Giorgis, galloping over the face of the earth on a soulless horse with a spear in hand, ready to fight the fearsome dragon. Now I knew that strength meant that if you fell off your horse, you walked. And if you could not walk any farther, you crawled until you could stand again.

My brother got to his feet and slowly climbed onto his mule. Negatwa scrambled up behind me. I liked knowing she was there at my back for whatever dangers lay ahead of us.

"We must begin," I said. A moment later, the sound of our mules' footsteps sent a song of soft thudding up to the star-filled sky.

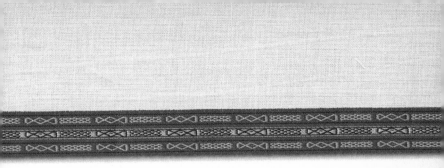

Then and Now ♦ *A Girl's Life*

E T H I O P I A

In the 1840s, when Saba's story takes place, Ethiopia was a land of sharp contrasts and fierce rivalries. High mountain peaks and scorching deserts, adorned palaces and peasant children begging for food, churches with rituals stretching back for thousands of years and deep-rooted beliefs in African spirits—all were part of Ethiopia, one of East Africa's largest countries.

For peasant children in the 1840s, childhood was brief and often dangerous. From the time they could barely walk, children like Saba and Mesfin worked on their small family farms, growing food and sometimes cotton. But hyenas and other wild animals threatened both livestock and people. Heavy taxation, over-

In the northern highlands, where Saba lived, most families lived in small, round houses with thatched, cone-shaped roofs. Families slept, cooked, and ate their meals in one room.

worked lands, and occasional long stretches of drought sometimes made food scarce. Soldiers sent by nobles to collect livestock or grain as taxes often looted and destroyed peasants' homes and fields. In the remote lowlands, there was also the threat of raiders who kidnapped children to sell them into slavery. According to one 19th-century traveler, three-fourths of the slaves in one caravan were young boys and girls, most of whom were girls under ten years old.

In the royal palaces at Gondar, Saba's life followed a very different tradition—the customs and rituals of nobility. Even her clothing reflected her new status. Saba's gold jewelry showed her royal lineage, since only members of the royal family could wear gold.

Gondar's royal palaces

A modern-day kemis

However, many Ethiopians wore amber, which varied in color from warm yellows to deep reds. The red umbrella held over Saba's head outdoors was also reserved for nobility. And her dress, or *kemis*, and matching shawl-like *shamma* were made of the finest cotton and were embroidered with shimmering silk.

Gondar was Ethiopia's largest city and the center of power. The city's markets drew people from all over Ethiopia. Merchants and farmers mixed with soldiers, priests, and the nobility. People from Ethiopia's many ethnic groups, including Amhara, Tigray, and Oromoo, all came together in Gondar.

Gondar was also home to 44 Orthodox churches, which were places of worship and education—and sanctuary to those in

*Many young Ethiopian women today still wear shammas, also called **netelas**, and carry their own colorful umbrellas to shield themselves from the sun.*

need. Orthodox Christianity, embraced by Ethiopian emperors in the fourth century, was the official religion of the land for more than fifteen hundred years.

The angels in this painting on the ceiling of a Gondar's Debre Birhan Selassie church have both eyes showing—a sign that they are "good souls."

Education was beyond the reach of most girls, except for some of noble birth. Sons of nobles sometimes attended church schools, while a few girls were tutored, as Saba was. Most girls, however, were expected to practice spinning and to prepare for marriage. In Saba's time, many girls were married before the age of 12—some as young as eight or nine. Parents arranged the marriage, often to a man the girl had never met.

An arranged marriage was not the only threat to Saba. The emperor, her great-uncle, was honored as the "King of Kings," descended from the Biblical Queen of Saba (or Queen of Sheba) and King Solomon.

All Ethiopian emperors have been descendants of the Queen of Saba.

Yet he had no real power. By the 1840s, the Ethiopian empire was divided into several kingdoms at war with each other. Saba's royal blood put her at the center of a murderous battle for control of the throne.

This tumultuous era is often called the "Age of Judges," after a time in the Old Testament book of Judges when "there was no king and every man did what was right in his own eyes." The confusing time came to an end in 1855, when a Robin Hood-like warrior named Kassa defeated the rulers of the other regions. He became Emperor Tewodros II, one of the three major rulers of 19th-century Ethiopia. Ethiopia's last emperor, Haile Selassie, was overthrown by the military in 1974. Today, the country is governed by elected officials.

If Saba were to walk into Ethiopia's capital city of Addis Ababa today, she would find the same rich mix of ethnic backgrounds, languages, and religions that once filled the royal city of Gondar. More than one hundred different ethnic groups, speaking over 80

Villagers attending a health education class in rural Ethiopia today

different languages, live in Ethiopia today.

For girls in rural areas today, life has changed little since Saba's time. In the cities, however, many have the opportunity to attend school, play sports, and eventually pursue careers. Still, traditions remain strong.

Today, the ancient, complex country of Ethiopia faces many problems. Years of civil war and deforestation, along with periodic droughts, have left behind widespread poverty. As Ethiopians struggle to rebuild their country, they know that their future depends on their children— children who will rely on their rich heritage, deep faith, and persistent courage to meet the challenges that lie ahead.

Modern Ethiopian girls

Glossary

Amharic has its own sound system, which is hard to reproduce in English, so these pronunciations are approximate.

ababba *(ah-buh-bah)*—father, also often used for grandfather or grandpa

amba *(ahm-bah)*—flat-topped mountain

Amhara *(ahm-hahr-ah)*—ethnic group of most of the Ethiopian emperors

ayezosh *(eye-zohsh)*—"Have courage"

azmari *(ahz-mah-ree)*—traveling musician

berebaso *(beh-reh-bah-so)*—Oromoo word for sandals

buda *(boo-dah)*—one believed to have evil, magical, powers

dik-dik *(deek-deek)*—smallest of the antelopes

doro *(doh-roh)*—chicken

emama *(eh-mah-mah)*—mother, also often used for grandmother or grandma

gahbi *(gah-bee)*—a thick cotton cloak

gebeta *(guh-buh-tuh)*—a game, also called "mancala"

Ge'ez *(gee-eez)*—ancient language of Ethiopia, still used in the Ethiopian Orthodox church

injera *(ihn-jeh-rah)*—pancake-like bread

kosso *(koh-soh)*—a kind of tree, parts of which are used to make a medication for stomach ailments

lalibelotch *(lah-lih-behl-ohch)*—dawn singers

masinko *(mah-sin-koh)*—musical instrument

Maskal *(muhs-kuhl)*—festival day near the end of our month of September

Maskaram *(mahs-kah-rahm)*—a month corresponding approximately to our September 12 to October 11

megebgeb *(meh-guhb-guhb)*—respectful wrap of the shamma

melkam addis amet *(mehl-kahm ah-dees ah-meht)*—"Good New Year"

negusa negst *(neh-goo-sah neh-gihst)*—"King of Kings"

Oromoo *(oh-roh-moo)*—large ethnic group of Ethiopia

shamma *(shah-mah)*—thin cotton shawl, also called "netala" *(neh-teh-lah)*

Tigray *(tih-gray)*—ethnic group traditionally living in the northern part of Ethiopia

wanza *(wahn-zah)*—a kind of tree

wat *(wuht)*—spicy stew

zar *(zahr)*—a spirit

Pronunciation of names and places:

Ali Alula (*ah-lee ah-loo-lah*)—powerful Gondar general

Berutawit (*beh-root-ah-wiht*)—literally "a girl from Beirut"

Debre Birhan Selassie (*dehb-rah bihr-hahn sehl-ah-see*)—"Mount of the Light of the Trinity," a church near Gondar

Debre Sahai (*dehb-rah ts-hi*)—"Mount of the Sun," a church near Gondar

Dembya (*dehmb-yah*)—a large lake in northwestern Ethiopia now named Lake Tana

Eslam Bet (*ehs-lahm beh-et*)—House of Islam

Fasiladas (*fah-sih-lah-dehs*)—emperor who founded Gondar

Fasil Gemb (*fah-sihl gehmb*)—castle built for Fasiladas

Giorgis (*jee-ohr-gis*)—George, a saint often found in ancient Ethiopian paintings

Gondar (*gohn-dahr*)—one of the ancient capitals of Ethiopia, located in northwestern Ethiopia

Kassa (*kah-sah*)—man eventually crowned Emperor Tewodros II, literally "compensation"

Makeda (*mah-keh-dah*)—name of the girl who, in

Ethiopian tradition, became Queen of Saba (Sheba)

Mariam (*mah-ree-ahm*)—Mary, mother of Jesus

Mekelle (*meh-kel-eh*)—town in northern Ethiopia

Menen (*meh-nehn*)—empress and wife of Yohannes III, and mother of Ali Alula

Mesfin (*mehs-fihn*)—Saba's brother, literally "prince"

Mikael (*mee-kye-ehl*)—Michael, a powerful 1700s general in Gondar

Negatwa (*neh-gah-twah*)—Saba's servant and friend, literally "the coming of dawn"

Saba (*sah-bah*)—Sheba, an ancient kingdom in what is now Yemen and northern Ethiopia

Suviel (*soo-vee-ehl*)—name of a legendary war horse

Tekle (*tehk-leh*)—former emperor and Saba's ancestor

Wallata Giorgis (*wah-lah-tah jee-ohr-gis*)—baptismal name of former empress who built the empress castle

Wehni (*weh-nee*)—amba where royalty was imprisoned

Yared (*yah-rehd*)—Jarad, an Ethiopian saint

Yesus Cristo (*yeh-zoos krees-tohs*)—Jesus Christ

Yohannes (*yoh-hahn-ness*)—John

Yosef (*yoh-sehf*)—Joseph, father of Jesus

Author's Note

My parents moved to Ethiopia when I was only two, and I spent most of my childhood there. When I was about twelve, I first saw the castles of Gondar and the angels on the ceiling of the church at Debre Birhan.

In Addis Ababa, the modern capital of Ethiopia, it was thrilling to catch glimpses of Emperor Haile Selassie, the last King of Kings, and to visit the lions caged near his palace.

My closest brush with royalty happened because I was in an accident near Gondar. A princess who ran a castle-turned-hotel helped my parents get medical attention for me. When Emperor Haile Selassie was deposed, most of his family was jailed—including this princess. Years later, after the princess was released, she told my mother, "I prayed for your daughter every day when I was in prison."

I made up Saba and her family, including her royal grandmother. But the other characters are taken from Ethiopian history and observations made by travelers. One European traveler described Empress Menen this way: "Greedy, miserly, clever, violent, ambitious, despotic, vain, coquettish, she stopped at nothing." Not long after this fictional story ends, the real Kassa captured the empress. Since she was his wife's grandmother, he did not want to harm her, but he forced her to grind grain until her aristocratic hands became rough as a peasant's hands. When Kassa finally became emperor, he was known as Emperor Tewodros, and he made the monarchy strong again.

After 20 years away from Ethiopia, I've recently returned several times to speak in international schools, to climb Maji mountain, and to help a librarian friend, Yohannes Gebregeorgis, establish a book center. I revisited Gondar and again tried to count the angels on the ceiling of the church. Sadly, I also saw the ongoing animosity between the Oromoo, Amhara, and other ethnic groups. Ethiopia has yet to believe its own proverb that when spiders unite, they can tie up a lion.

Jane Kurtz